www.S

Marrying My Childhood Sweetheart

She left her childhood sweetheart, but now wants him back...

A complete Christian romance for adults, brought to you by Shannon Gardener of BWWM Club.

Sara and David were childhood sweethearts.

But while things had been perfect between them for so long, Sara soon began feeling she needed more out of life.

So leaving David and her family behind, she went out to search for adventure in the big city.

www.SaucyRomanceBooks.com/RomanceBooks

But as many have found out, the grass isn't always greener on the other side.

Soon discovering she has made a mistake, she returns to her previous life and tries to reconnect with David, the only man she's ever really wanted to marry.

But does David still feel the same about her?

And can Sara do what's needed to rekindle the love of a lifetime?

Find out in this touching Christian marriage romance by Shannon Gardener of BWWM Club (search us).

Suitable for over 18s only due to sex scenes between a loving Christian couple.

Warning: this story contains sex before marriage.

Tip: Search **BWWM Club** on Amazon to see more of our great books.

www.SaucyRomanceBooks.com/RomanceBooks

Get Free Romance eBooks!

Hi there. As a special thank you for buying this book, for a limited time I want to send you some great ebooks completely **free of charge** directly to your email! You can get it by going to this page:

www.saucyromancebooks.com/physical

You can see a the cover of these books on the next page:

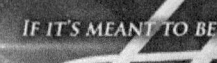

www.SaucyRomanceBooks.com/RomanceBooks

www.SaucyRomanceBooks.com/RomanceBooks

These ebooks are so exclusive you can't even buy them. When you download them I'll also send you updates when new books like this are available.

Again, that link is:

www.saucyromancebooks.com/physical

ISBN-13: 978-1516890972

ISBN-10: 1516890973

Copyright © 2015 to Shannon Gardener and SaucyRomanceBooks.com. No part of this book can be copied or distributed without written permission from the above copyright holders.

www.SaucyRomanceBooks.com/RomanceBooks

Contents

Chapter 1 - Page 7

Chapter 2 - Page 24

Chapter 3 - Page 39

Chapter 4 - Page 60

Chapter 5 - Page 75

Chapter 6 - Page 94

Chapter 7 - Page 112

Chapter 8 - Page 131

Chapter 9 - Page 149

Chapter 10 - Page 167

Get Free Romance eBooks - Page 184

More Books By Shannon Gardener - Page 187

www.SaucyRomanceBooks.com/RomanceBooks

Chapter 1

Sara applied her make-up with painstaking care; her movement methodical. She had chosen charcoal gray for the eye shadow ; she had always been told that it brought out the gold flecks in her dark brown eyes and made them look bigger than their normal size. She needed to look her best because she would be facing the people she had run out four years ago. Twenty seemed a hundred years ago and she felt like she had grown up so much in those years. Next, she applied the rose lip gloss, which highlighted her full pouty lips. She passed a hand over her short cropped hair, sometimes it felt so strange to her not to have the familiar curls brushing against her shoulders but she had acquired this look when she had been in the big city and it suited her small heart shaped face. Apart from looking a little thin she guessed she looked all right, not the worst for wear, she thought grimly.

There was a discreet knock on her room door which was partially open. It was her father and he looked at her gently, good old Dad, or Deacon Williams as he was known fondly to those at church – no judgment dad as he was known to her. "Ready to face the cavalry?" he asked teasingly. He was already dressed in his old fashioned tweed suit and broad red tie; his salt and pepper hair brushed ruthlessly back from his lined chocolate colored face.

She had wanted to stay home and bury herself in self-pity but her father had told her gently but firmly that she was going to have to face people sooner or later and sooner sounded a lot better. He had told her that our mistakes do not define who we are and as long as we learn from them, then we are on our way. "Not quite," she told him wryly, "But I am hoping to garner strength along the way," She stood up and brushed down her black and white dress with the flared waist; a red belt cinched in her small waist.

"That's the spirit and you always look beautiful, can't get used to your hair being so short though," he told her with a little frown.

"You'll get used to it," she told him cheerfully, walking over to him, red earrings dangling at her lobes. "Let's go," she looped her hand on his arm and they went downstairs together. The house was old but charming and had been in the Williams' family for three generations. Her Dad had added a porch, complete with a swing and had done little renovations here and there. He had moved out of the master bedroom when her mother had left them when she was only seven years old and had taken a smaller bedroom several doors down from hers.

They went in his old Chevrolet that had seen better days. Her car was a little red sport car and was not appropriate, nor the right fit for her father anyway. She was going back to church where she had been so active before she left; a Sunday school teacher and an organizer of the youth department and she had left her friends and church family without even saying goodbye; now she was back home to face them and she was quaking inside. They were all going to witness how much she had failed; not quite the success she had thought she was going to be.

"Don't worry, my dear, people can be very forgiving," her father said kindly, reaching over to give her hand a pat. "Soon they will be welcoming you back inside the fold."

Sara smiled but did not respond.

When they reached the church, people were milling outside, getting ready to go but as was the usual procedure; they had to catch up on what had happened since the last time they met. This was what had annoyed her before she left and it was what she had come to miss when she was away. How ironic life was, she thought wryly. She knew that practically everyone knew she was back home even though she was only home from Friday. She had seen the elderly Sister Thorpe who did housework for her dad and she was the church's grapevine.

She found herself searching; ignoring the eyes on her as her father took her hand and they walked through the yard; greeting people politely but not stopping to engage in conversation; time enough for that later. She did not see him; at least not until she had gotten inside the building and her heart turned right over in her chest. There he was; on the pulpit with the other choristers; he was director of the choir now; her father had told her. David Graham; the man she had left broken hearted on her quest to seek something better for her life. He was still so achingly handsome and as Sara stared at him furtively she saw him laugh at something Holly McKenzie said to him; his white smile flashing. She looked away quickly; not wanting him to notice her staring; she had moved on and she was sure he had too.

She sat in the back seat, near to the exit – it was a small church and everyone knew each other. Parents came out with their children and the tradition continued so the familiarity was kept constant. That was what she had wanted to escape – she had wanted anonymity – for a while.

The service was conducted by the same Pastor, Leroy Phillips and he was still going strong even though he had to be close to seventy now. Her father had gone on up front to sit near the pulpit in case he was needed. She remembered days gone by when she had been so eager to reach church; not only to be with David but also to meet up with her friends and how in love with Jesus she had been. Her best friend then had been Callie and looking up front she saw her – she was married to Brother Paul Blake now and have a son. She had not kept in touch with her either and Sara knew there was a lot of hurt there; and fences that needed mending; but not now; first she had to concentrate on her own healing.

The message was ironically about the prodigal son and Sara was sure the whole congregation was staring at her; she wanted to flee but resolutely stayed and listened; her eyes glued to the Pastor. He spoke about accepting those who had gone astray and welcoming them back with open arms, as our Father in heaven does to us.

Then it was time for the choir to sing. Sara stared mesmerized as David took the lead; his clear baritone ringing out the first verse. He had always been a magnificent singer but seemed to have honed the skill over the years. He sounded like an angel.

She was the first one to exit the church as soon as the service ended; swiftly going over to the car to wait for her father. That was where Callie found her. She was by herself and Sara saw that her husband and son were talking with a group of people.

"Hi Sara," Callie's voice was cool and remote as if she was speaking to a stranger. The girl had put on a little weight but was still wholesomely pretty with curly shoulder length hair and large dark eyes; her caramel colored skin smooth and unlined.

"Hi Callie," Sara ventured a smile. "I see you have started a family."

"Yes," she looked over to where they were, a smile on her face which vanished instantly as she turned to face her one time friend. "I never expected you to come back."

"I never expected to," Sara shrugged, her eyes moving past her friend to look aimlessly around. She was not ready for this; it was too soon. "I did a lot of things I am sorry for and I know maybe you won't believe me but I am so sorry,"

"I will get over it," she told her; looking at her critically. "I am sure you have learnt from your mistake and if the good Lord can forgive you who am I not to?"

Sara stared at her in amusement, "I see you are rearing to take over from Pastor Phillips," she teased. "When did you become so preachy?"

Callie laughed ruefully, the mood lightening. "Since I have become a wife and mother," she admitted sheepishly. "Welcome back," she gave Sara a surprise hug and after a brief hesitation Sara returned it with relief – at least she had two people in her corner, her father and Callie.

Her father was approaching and with him was Pastor Phillips. Sara's heart sank; she just wanted to leave and she was regretting not driving her car. "Give them time," Callie told her softly, giving her hand a squeeze, "By the way, you look sensational," she added. "I will call you," she went on her way greeting Deacon Williams and Pastor Phillips.

"My dear it is so good to see you," Pastor Phillips enveloped her in a big hug, smelling as usual of peppermint and assurance. "Happy to have you back and if there's anything you need to talk about, you know my door is always open."

"Thanks Pastor," she told him quietly as he released her. It was as if he had opened the way for the others; by the time he had finished talking to her, several people came over and welcomed her back; saying they were glad to see her.

Sara escaped shortly after, her heart racing, wondering if any minute she would see David at her side and she did not know quite what to say to him. Her father gently told them they had to leave and they drove away without seeing him.

"I told you it wouldn't be so bad," he smiled at her as they made their way home.

"And you were right," Sara said, settling back against the faded leather seat with a sigh. "When are you going to get rid of this gas guzzler dad?"

"Old Betsy is here to stay young lady," he told her with a twinkle in his eyes. "And I am sure she does not appreciate you referring to her as a gas guzzler."

Sara laughed and for the first time since she had been back; she felt as if things were going to work out.

They had dinner in the small living room. Her father had made his famous fried chicken and potato salad and she ate with gusto. "Are you trying to fatten me up?" she teased as he put some more potato salad on her plate.

"You could do with a little more meat on those bones," he told her looking at her speculatively.

"Dad," she protested halfheartedly, putting some of the delicious salad into her mouth. "I would have you know that this is an ideal weight for my height."

"Nonsense," he waved a hand at her. "A little more flesh won't kill you."

They finished eating in companionable silence and Sara cleared the table and told him she would do the washing up. He retired to his study to read his Bible and maybe to pray. Sara took the opportunity to go and finish the unpacking and sort out her room. He had left the room the same way since she had been away; not moving anything but making sure it was neat and tidy. She had changed out all her girlish furniture when she turned eighteen and had gone with a bold design – splashes of red and blue everywhere. She wandered over to the dressing table where there was still a photo of her and David that had been taken at the fair; the summer before she left.

Her hair had been shoulder length then and the breeze had whipped it around his face and she had been looking up at him and him staring down at her. They had looked so happy together until she had decided that she wanted more for herself. How wrong she had been.

She was about to place the photo back on the dresser but she put it in a drawer instead – she needed no reminders of her past; even though she was right back in the middle it.

*****

Monday morning dawned bright and with it the promise of a new start. She had decided to accept her father's offer and help him run the bookstore. She had worked there every summer when she was a teenager and helped him set up the internet café as well; he had been so pleased that she had shown an interest in the 'family business' as he referred to it until she had left; telling him that working in a bookstore was not her life's dream.

He had left right after breakfast; telling her that he had some books to sort out and she should take her time. He had prepared pancakes and eggs but she had shuddered at the heaping of syrup and whipped cream and decided she would have black coffee and a plain bagel. Her father looked as if he was making good on his desire to fatten her up, she thought wryly. She sat in the small homely kitchen sipping her coffee thoughtfully. There was still some evidence of her mother around. The coffee maker she had bought on one of her visits in town; the garish table cloth on the kitchen table and the marble counter top she had replaced the Formica one for. Thinking about her mother had gotten less and less depressing as the years went by and the pain of her abandonment had dulled considerably; the sense of betrayal remained though and she wondered how her father managed to keep it together all these years.

Shaking her head as if to get rid of the troubling thoughts, she stood and washed out her coffee cup – her father was not very tolerant when it came to dirty sinks. She had dressed for her first day back in cream pants and a teal cotton blouse; the time was a little nippy even though it was the middle of summer; so she had added a black lightweight jacket as well. Gold knobs winked at her ear lobes and she had put on matching bracelets. She got there at a quarter to nine and her father was already busy with customers. He looked up with a smile and waved her over. Sara hurriedly went inside the small office and put away her pocket book and the coffee she had carried with her; before going out to join her father.

He left at noon and said he had a meeting with a bookseller and he would be gone for at least an hour.

The bookstore was empty when he came in. She had just sat down to drink her warmed up coffee when she heard the tinkle of the doorbell. It was David and she felt as if she was glued to the chair; it was him and her heart was thundering so much inside her that she hardly heard the greeting.

"Sara," his voice; that deep husky baritone that always had the power to weaken her. He was dressed in faded jeans and a black T-shirt that exposed his tanned hairy arms.

"David," she murmured, standing at last on legs that threatened to betray her.

"I wanted to see your dad, is he here? I don't see his car out front." He slowly came towards her.

"He – he went to a meeting," she cursed herself for the uncertainty in her voice.

"I didn't get a chance to welcome you back yesterday at church, by the time I came out you were already gone." He stood a few feet away from her. "How are you?"

"I am doing great." she said with bravado.

"You've changed your hair, it suits you," he smiled at her slightly.

"Thanks," she placed an unconscious over her short cropped hair. "How have you been?"

"Very well thank you," he told her soberly.

"David I am –" she began but he held up a hand to stop her.

"You did what you had to do Sara," he told her a little grimly.

"Yes I did," her pointed chin lifted and she squared her shoulders. If he did not want her apology then to hell with him.

He stared at her searchingly for a minute and then he said in a cool remote voice. "Please tell your father to call me, thanks." Without waiting for her to respond, he turned and left.

She stood there feeling as if the earth had just been dragged from under her and she was floating with nowhere to stop and nothing to anchor her. She did not blame him hating her. He had expressed his love for her so many times over the years and she had told him to give her time and he had done that and she had gone ahead and left him with barely a goodbye. She remembered the day quite clearly as if it was yesterday.

She had called him over to the house and told him it was urgent and she did not want to speak about it over the phone.

At 22, David had been on the lanky side; his dark hair having a tendency to curl. She had often teased him that he looked more like a girl than she did with that head of beautiful hair and long lashes.

He had been at church, rehearsing but had left to rush over to see her.

"Hey what's up?" he had asked as soon as she let him inside. Her father was at the bookstore and she had pretended to be ill so she didn't have to go in. She had finished college and had gotten a degree in literature and had pondered on teaching but the enthusiasm was not there so her father had asked her to help him out until she decided what she needed to do.

She had been pacing the whole time till he got there and she still had no idea how to tell him. She had been secretly sending out head shots to the big city and had gotten a response. An agent was interested and wanted to sign her on. She had been a good Christian girl to please all around her and she was done with it – it was time to think about her for a change.

"I got an offer," she blurted out.

"An offer for what?" he asked her puzzled. He had been about to pull her into his arms and she evaded him. They had had sex for the first time for both of them when she turned eighteen and he considered her to be his girl.

"From a modeling agency, I want to be a model." She told him shakily. He stood there staring at her as if she had taken leave of her senses.

"What about us? About church? About your father?" he asked her bewildered.

"I will deal with my father later and church will always be there." She took a deep breath. "I have to do this David and if you love me you will be happy for me."

"Don't do that," he told her heatedly, advancing towards her. "I love you and I want to spend my life with you so don't expect me to be happy that you want to go."

"You don't know what love really is," she cried out in frustration, pulling away from him. "I don't want to stay in this backwater town for the rest of my life. I want to see what's out there and I want you to be happy for me."

There was silence for so long that Sara wondered if he was ever going to respond. Then he did. Reaching out he pulled her into his arms and took her lips with his; bruising her with his intensity. She dragged herself away from him; her breathing ragged. "I am going," she told him shakily. "So deal with it."

"I love you Sara but if you leave don't expect me to be here waiting for you." He told her quietly and slammed out of the house. She had cried herself to sleep; almost going after him but she had made up her mind; she had to escape and no one was going to talk her out of it. Now she was back and she had seen him and she realized with a dull thud of her heart that she still had feelings for him. How was she going to go around this small town without bumping into him? And what if he was seeing someone, how was she going to deal with it?

With a shudder, she gulped back tears and wished she had never come back.

Chapter 2

"I can see you are very busy, maybe I should come back later," Sally Graham commented as she came inside the green house where her son was busy placing seeds into the newly dug ground. The place smell of freshly dug dirt mixed with the heady scent of many different flowers. It never ceased to amaze her how her son had turned the place in a veritable forest.

"I am never too busy for my favorite mother," he told her cheerfully, pulling off his gardening gloves and coming over to kiss her on the cheek.

"Your only mother," she told him dryly. She had brought him lunch in a picnic basket because she knew when he was working he did not have time to eat and she also wanted to see how he was doing; due to Sara coming back to town. No matter how old he was, he was still her one and only baby.

"And you brought lunch," David observed, glancing at his wristwatch in surprise to see that it was almost noon. He had started working at six a.m. and had not stopped. He had not slept very well the night before. She was back and all the old feelings were stirring up inside him, seeing her at the bookstore yesterday and how incredibly beautiful she had grown had not made it easy on him.

"How are you?" she asked him bluntly, she was never one to beat around the bush. It always amazed her this giant of a man came from her petite frame but he had gotten the height from his father and the looks from her.

"I'm fine," he shrugged, going over to the small pipe to wash off the dirt before coming over to the table where his mother was seated with the intention of partaking of the food. He had set up the greenhouse in such a way that he could have somewhere he could eat and there was also an old hammock where if he felt like it, he could take a nap.

"Have you seen her?" Sally persisted as he reached for a chicken sandwich.

David thought about pretending he had no idea what or who she was referring to but knowing his mother; he decided against it. "I saw her yesterday," he said casually, no one; not even his mother whom he loved so much was going to know the extent of what he was going through in regards to Sara – that was between him and God.

"And?"

"And nothing mother," he said with a little impatience coloring his deep voice. "I went to the bookstore looking for Deacon Williams and she was there and we spoke briefly."

"So there was no apology or no explanation as to why she is back?" Sally was not letting up.

"Mom," David said wearily, placing the half eaten sandwich on the paper plate. "I don't want to talk about Sara; she is my past and I want to move on from it so please drop it."

"Darling, the fact that you are having a warm time talking about her means she is not your past and you are going to have to deal with it sooner or later." She stood up getting ready to leave. "You're still in love with her son and what you plan on doing with that is entirely up to you." She gave him a kiss and left. He sat there staring at nothing, his mother's words reverberating through him and with a sinking heart he knew it was true, he was still in love with her.

*****

Callie called her on Wednesday and suggested they had lunch. Sara had a moment of hesitation but she accepted; after all if she was going to mend fences, she had better go about it the right way.

She had not slept well on Monday night. She kept seeing David's face and what was worst, she kept remembering what he felt like when they were together all those years ago. She had been with one other person apart from him; the man she had thought could and would replace David in her heart but he had turned out to be a real jerk who had only wanted her as long as she appeared to be going places and when the agency had dropped her; he'd also told her that he didn't think it was going to work out between them.

They met for lunch at the little restaurant at the corner of the street down from the bookstore. She'd told her father she was going to get lunch and she would be back in the next half an hour. He had waved her away with a smile and told her to go and get out of the bookstore, stretch her legs a little.

The restaurant was a little crowded as it was lunch hour but Callie was already seated; her eyes brightening as soon as she saw Sara. "I have already ordered for you," she told her as Sara slid into the booth next to her.

"You did?" Sara raised a brow questioningly.

"I remember how much you used to like the chicken salad in this place," she answered, and then her brow creased uncertainly. "Unless of course, your tastes have changed."

"No of course not," Sara hastened to assure her.

"You look like you just stepped from the pages of a fashion magazine," Callie sighed, eyeing the girl's chic and graceful appearance. She had chosen to wear tailored black pants and a sleeveless red blouse with buttons at the front.

"One of the advantages of working in the modeling industry," Sara said with a wry smile.

"Why did you leave Sara?" Callie asked suddenly, there were the usual background noises in the restaurant, muted chatters, utensils banging against glassware but at the table the silence was evident.

"I had to get away," Sara answered finally, her large eyes sparkling with unshed tears. "I had to see what else was out there and I did not want to turn out like my mother who married my father and found out she could not cut it as a Deacon's wife and a stay at home mom. I could not do that to David."

"So instead you left and broke his heart in little pieces." Callie said grimly, shaking her head. "You were my best friend Sara and you did not share any of those things with me; you just left."

"I was not thinking straight," Sara told her miserably. "I just bolted without thinking of the consequences and what I was doing to the people I care about."

Just then their food arrived and further conversations ceased for a little bit.

"Is he seeing anyone?" Sara asked casually as she put some of the crunchy delicious salad into her mouth.

Callie looked at her speculatively, dipping her bread into her beef soup. "You still love him," she said shrewdly.

"No," Sara shook her head furiously.

"Then why are you asking?"

"I am just hoping he's found someone; that's all," Sara was busy sprinkling salt on her salad and avoiding Callie's eyes.

"He was going out with Patrice for a little bit but it's been over for a while now," Callie told her. "You might have gone for several years Sara but I still know you. You're still in love with David and for you to be feeling that way about him still, means that he is the one. You will have to find a way of getting back with him."

Sara opened her mouth to deny everything the closed it abruptly – she did not know what to say because Callie was right – she was still in love with him.

"So you're married to Paul," Sara commented, changing the subject.

"Yes, he would not stop asking so I just had to say yes," Callie told her with a wicked grin. Sara was taken back to when they had been teenagers and Callie had always been the one daring her to try out new things. Callie had always been there for her; encouraging her when her mother had left – she had adopted Callie's mother and had gone to her when she needed advice. And the woman had died a year ago and she had not even come back home for the funeral. She hated herself for what she did.

"I am sorry about Mommy Paulette," Sara murmured ducking her head in shame.

"She talked about you so much, often praying that you would find your way," Callie told her soberly. "She never hated you, Sara," she reached out a hand to close over Sara's. "She loved you till the end; always saying she had two daughters, not one. And even when I was cussing you out, she always told me you had to have had a very good reason for leaving."

"She was always such a beautiful person," Sara said huskily, the tears threatening. "I often found myself wishing that she had been my mother instead of – you know." She gave a shrug.

"You can't blame yourself for what your mother did Sara, it's all on her." Callie said sympathetically. "It's her loss."

"Thanks," Sara smiled and squeezed the girl's hand. "You're your mother's daughter."

Callie smiled at her and they continued eating.

Sara left soon after, exclaiming in surprise to know that she had gone over the half hour she had told her father and with a quick wave she told the other girl she would call her.

*****

Her father was stocking books when she got back. "Dad, why didn't you leave that for me to do?" she rushed over and took the box from him.

"I am not an old doddering man that I cannot manage a box of books girl," he reproached her with a fond smile.

"I know it's just that I want to pull my weight around here," she told him sheepishly. There was only a teenage girl sitting in the corner on the computer, a text book opened in front of her.

"You are," he glanced at her shrewdly. "You don't have to prove anything to me you know Sara. You are my daughter and I have no judgment or opinion as to why you left. I accept you for who you are."

"Thanks Dad," she said huskily, tears clogging her throat.

"That young man David has some books he wants delivered and I was wondering if you would save an old man the trip and take them over to his place. He writes for the local newspaper and he needs some books to do his work."

Sara fought the impulse to shout out no. She could not face him at his place; she didn't even know where he lived.

"The address is on the parcel right there," Her father told her as if reading her thoughts.

She had to go; there was no getting out of it.

*****

She got to the address and sat in her car for several minutes. It was a nice place; as a matter of fact it was more than that – it was beautiful and the garden was rioting with summer flowers, he always did love nature, she thought with a whimsical smile. The house was set back a little from the road and it was a simple one story building with stucco roof. She could see the green house; a large building with glass all around it and she caught a glimpse of him inside.

Taking a deep breath, she alighted from the car with his package and headed towards the white picket fence. She stood there uncertainly for a while wondering if she should just go on in. The decision was made for her as she saw him come out and stood there staring at her before he beckoned for her to come in. Her heels were not appropriate for the uneven ground and Sara found herself stepping gingerly until she reached him. "Your father called and said you were coming," he told her. He was in faded jeans and an old T-shirt and there was a smudge of dirt on his cheek. "Come on in," he told her; heading back inside. Sara gritted her teeth and followed him; she had wanted to just give him the package and leave.

The interior of the greenhouse took her breath away and Sara found herself breathing in the aroma. There were vegetables of all description and they looked so healthy. "This is nice," she murmured.

"Thank you," he murmured in amusement, his eyes taking in her outfit. "You're not exactly dressed for this," he waved a hand at the bags of soil near her.

"Not exactly," she agreed.

"I'm surprised you offered to bring the package to me," he continued, his eyes quizzical.

"I did not offer, I was told," she told him coolly.

"I see," he put aside the trowel and turned to face her, leaning against the table filled with seedlings. "Afraid I am going to pick up where we left off?"

"Don't be ridiculous," she avoided his eyes.

"Yes, that would be ridiculous wouldn't it?" he walked over to her. Sara forced herself to remain where she was. "You left me and broke my heart in two, so it would be ridiculous of me to want to have anything to do with you. Only a fool would venture where the greatest hurt has been done to him, don't you think?"

"David I-" she hated herself for showing signs of weakness.

"What are you going to say Sara? You're sorry? You didn't mean to hurt me? You're sorry that when you left I could not function for months; no years? Is that what you want to say?" He was too near, she thought in panic, so near that she could smell the fresh dirt and spicy cologne he always used. He was so near that she could feel his breath on her.

"I need to leave," she was not breathing properly.

"So go ahead and leave, I am not holding you," he still stood in front of her and she could not move. "Do you want to?" he asked her huskily. "Or do you want to know what it feels like again? To feel my lips on yours?"

"No," she whispered, her eyes on his mouth.

"You were pretty before, but now you're so damned beautiful it hurts the eyes." He reached up a hand and pushed back a curl that had blown unto her forehead. "When you left I wanted to die; I kept thinking about you being with someone else and I couldn't bear it, I didn't sleep and I wanted to come and find you, to convince you we belong together and I would do anything you wanted." His tone was mesmerizing and Sara found herself trembling. "Your lips always drove me crazy and they still do," he murmured huskily as he tilted her chin to look into her eyes; eyes that had gone smoky gray with need. "You broke me and I still want you; there must be something wrong with me." His lips came down as if in slow motion and Sara's lips parted in anticipation. He took her lips with his; his mouth moving hers slowly; his tongue delving inside her mouth. He tasted of peppermint and candy, an odd combination but he secretly had a sweet tooth and could not resist sweets. She touched him, her hand going to his chest which had hardened with manual labor and she felt his muscles flexing. She whimpered softly and sagged into his arms; wanting more, needing more but with a savage oath he pushed her away from him; combing his hands through his hair.

"Go," he told her through gritted teeth.

"David?" her voice was bewildered as she put a finger to her throbbing lips.

"Just go Sara, please," he muttered wearily, his back still turned to her, his shoulders hunched. "I can't do this, not now."

Sara left on shaky legs and when she reached the car she got in and just sat there; her hands on the steering wheel; her heart was still pounding and she could not put the car in drive. She needed time to calm down; time to settle herself before going back to the bookstore. She still felt him; his mouth on hers –he was the only man who could turn her to jelly with just a kiss. He hated her and she couldn't blame him but now she realized with a thud, she would do anything to right the wrong she had done him. He was no longer the sweet David she had known who had allowed her to walk all over him; the David who had told her constantly that he would do anything for her. The David who had told her everything about him.

She fired up the engine and drove off, her mind in a turmoil; she remembered how excited she had been when she had gotten her first modeling gig and how confident she had been that she was going to make it big and then she had met Michael who had seemed so glamorous and confident with his three piece suit and tie and his fancy apartment and the way he took her out to fancy restaurants. She had been so caught up with the sophistication that she never saw him for who he really was – she had been such a fool. She had left a wonderful life in a small town and the love of a wonderful man to go off and gotten involved in a life, so superficial and meaningless. She parked the car a little distance away from the bookstore, staring at a couple holding hands and crossing the road. The man said something and the girl laughed and hugged him. She'd had that with David and she had not been satisfied and now it was gone from her. Sara felt the tears coming and she did not stop them; until she realized they were pouring down in torrents and her shoulders were shaking with the sobs racking her body.

Chapter 3

She barely got through the rest of the week and every time the doorbell sounded, she looked up expecting to see David.

Sunday came with dark angry clouds and a humidity that defied description. She pretended to be ill when her father asked her about going to church. She knew she was taking the coward's way out but she could not bear the thought of facing David just yet. And besides, she wanted to be by herself for a little bit.

"Make sure you get yourself something to eat," he told her sternly as he brought her some herbal tea and a slice of toast. Sara felt a little guilty as she told him thanks but it was worth it just to have the time to herself to think and to plan. He left shortly after and Sara drank the tea, leaving the bread untouched, sliding the sheet over her; burrowing her head on the pillows. He had kissed her and she had let him; not only that but she had wanted it so badly and had wanted so much more.

The memories kept flooding back. The time when he had made a picnic lunch for them and they had stolen out after their parents had gone to bed; and he had brought a blanket along and a pillow. She had just turned nineteen and he said he wanted to celebrate with her alone. There had been a huge cypress tree in the nearby park. The night had been cool and he had brought all kinds of sandwiches and a bottle of cheap wine.

They had eaten their full and had drank the whole bottle of wine and had laid there staring up at the stars, slightly inebriated.

"I wish we could stay this way for a while," she murmured as she linked her hand in his.

"We can," he told her softly, rolling over to hover over her. "I love you," he had told her passionately. "And I want to be with you every single day." He had not waited for her to respond but had bent his head and kissed her; his inexperienced kisses stirring her heart.

They had fallen asleep and jumped up before dawn; hurrying home before they were missed.

They had talked about so many things but she had never told him her yearning to become a model; he had always assumed she was satisfied to just stay in the little place where they were born and that they would get married eventually. She had tried to be what everyone wanted her to be but she had wanted to do more, see more and she had but it just had not turned out the way she expected.

She fell asleep shortly after and it was not until her Dad came home that she realized she had spent almost the entire morning in bed. She hurriedly got up and went to the bathroom to take a shower. She could hear him downstairs hanging up his raincoat and umbrella and she quickly pull on a pair of shorts and an old T-shirt. She was not in the mood for questions right now. He came upstairs just as she was heading down and he stopped halfway.

"How are you feeling?" the concern was evident in his voice.

"Not too bad now," Sara continued down. "I guess I just needed to get some rest."

"Good," he kissed her on the cheek as she made to pass him.

"How was church?" she asked him

"Very good, your friend Callie asked after you and of course young David asked if you were okay," he gave her a questioning look which she ignored.

"Okay, I'll just rustle us up some dinner," she turned to go inside the kitchen. "How do feel about a chicken salad?"

"Sounds good," he told her; going upstairs.

They ate at the kitchen table with her father telling her about the sermon preached at church.

"Dad may I ask you something?" she asked him as he drank down a glass of root beer.

"Of course," he told her, looking at her curiously. He was almost sixty and there were patches of gray in his thick dark hair that he wore very low but apart from that he looked a lot younger.

"Do you still love her?" she had always wanted to ask him that question but had been so afraid of bringing up the hurt and pain he must still be feeling.

He put his empty glass carefully on the coaster; careful lest he made a water ring on the lovingly polished mahogany.

"I will always love her," he told her quietly, with a sad smile.

"But why?" Sara cried, shaking her head in bewilderment. "She left you, left us and without a word and has not been back or even being in touch, what's there to love?"

"You can't just turn off love like that Sara, I hope you know that," he stared at her quizzically. "I loved your mother for a long time and that's not going to change, no matter what she did. Our Lord Jesus loves us no matter how many times we mess up and nothing we do will ever make Him stop loving us. Caroline left because she could not handle a small town and what it took to be wife to a deacon and the responsibilities it entails. I can't hate her, my dear because that would mean I never loved her in the first place."

That was probably the longest speech she had ever heard from her father and Sara found herself staring at this magnificent man who in spite of his heartbreak and pain had brought her up in the best way possible.

"I can't forgive her," Sara murmured, looking away from him.

"That's up to you my dear," her father reached out and took her hands in his. "But not forgiving her means that you are missing out on life and you're letting her have power over you. You're too beautiful; inside and out to live life halfheartedly."

"Don't you hate her just a little bit?" Sara asked pleadingly, holding on to his hands.

Deacon Williams laughed fondly, squeezing her hands. "Not even a little bit. We both made something wonderful and that's you by the way and for that I will forever be grateful; everything else pales beside that; I actually feel sorry for her and what she has missed, watching you grow up."

"Have you heard from her?" Sara asked him, her eyes lighting up at how proud he was of her.

"Several years after she left, she called; telling me how sorry she was and she had met someone and she was planning to get married." He smiled a little whimsically. "She wanted my forgiveness and the assurance that I would not say anything to you about her to make you hate her."

Sara was silent for a spell then she looked at him. "And you never remarry," she commented.

"Not because of her but because of you, my dear." He told her. "I would never allow another woman to try and play mother to you and I was contented to let it just be you and I."

"Oh Daddy," Sara reverted to her childhood name for him and coming around the table, she hugged him tightly. "I love you so much." She whispered.

"I love you too, my little girl." He told her huskily.

That night when she went to bed, she lay awake thinking about what her father had said to her and how serene and peaceful he was. She had been so angry for so long and she was getting tired of feeling that way – she knew she wanted a change.

*****

"My dear you are just the person I wanted to see," Pastor Phillips greeted her warmly. He had come into the bookstore and she was just about to tell him that her father was on the road. She had gone to church last week Sunday and had not seen David; Callie had told her he had gone to a visiting church to do a performance. She had not seen him in two weeks and to her despair, she found that she wanted to see him so much that she kept looking up whenever the doorbell tinkled; expecting it to be him.

She waited until he told her what he wanted from her. She had known Pastor Phillips since she was a little girl and had grown to realize that when he wanted something done; he did not ask, he charmingly suggested.

"I remember you were involved with the youth department and we have a function coming up for next Sunday; some concert or the other," he waved a hand vaguely. "Brother David has suggested we hold a concert in order to raise some much needed funds for the department. We have young people going back to school and all that and they need the monetary help. He is having a meeting with them tomorrow and we would very much appreciate you being there." At the name of David, she had stopped listening and she knew she would refuse; but she had never been able to say no to Pastor Phillips; no one ever had and she did not know how to start now.

"That's tomorrow," she told him weakly. The store had emptied a short while ago so they were sitting at the corner table.

"Yes my dear, short notice I know but I am sure you'll make it." He patted her hand fondly and stood up to leave. "Tell Deacon I will speak to him later concerning Sunday." With a wave he left, leaving Sara staring after him in bewilderment. She had committed to something and she had no idea when she had done so.

*****

Sara dressed carefully the next day. She had planned on going to church straight from work and she was determined to look her best; it was a matter of pride, she thought grimly, pulling on a slim fitting green cotton skirt and a sleeveless green and yellow silk blouse. She added green accessories and black pumps. Her hair had grown somewhat since she had been back and it fell in lustrous wave over her forehead.

The store was very busy and before she knew it; it was time to leave. "Dad I will see you later at home," she picked up her pocket book from the office and headed for the door.

"Be safe," he told her with a smile and went back to the cash register where he was ringing up a sale.

There was no other car in the parking lot when she got there and at first she thought she was early; she knew David drove a pickup truck that he used to make deliveries in and it was nowhere to be seen. Just as she was about to get out of the car, she saw the side door opened and he came out. Her heart thudded inside her; it was actually good to see him. He was wearing blue slacks and a blue dress shirt which was opened at the neck, revealing a glimpse of dark chest hair.

"I see you're right on time," he said, coming to stand beside the car. "Nice wheels," he murmured appreciatively, running a hand over the shiny red surface.

"Thanks," she murmured. "Where are the others?"

"The young people will be here shortly, so let's go inside. I want to discuss some of the plans I have for the concert." He opened her door for her and she stepped out, she could not help but notice his eyes on her bare legs.

He preceded her and held the door open for her. They were in the large church hall and Sara remembered the many times she and David and several others had stayed until way into the night to practice some play or songs or just hang out and quizzed each other on upcoming tests at school – it had been their hang out spot and at one point, where they had cuddled and kissed when the others had left. Sara stole a look at him to see if he remembered but he had gone up to where the music was.

"It looks the same," she murmured, looking around at all the empty seats.

"Except for the addition of a keyboard," he pointed to the corner. "It's the same."

He took a seat and invited her to join him. With a slight hesitation, she did; staying far away from him.

"I won't bite, Sara," he told her in amusement. "Not unless you invite me to," his tone changed to one of huskiness. He stared at her and she stared back, mesmerized by his dark brown eyes. It was the babble of voices coming inside the door that broke the spell.

He got up and took charge, leaving her rooted to the bench, trying to gather her wits. With a deep breath she rose and joined him as he spoke to the young members.

He wanted a concert with a difference. There would be the usual singing but he wanted to depict some of the gospel reading in dramatic prose. And he wanted dances as well. The meeting went off without a hitch and with a feeling of great anticipation they made a date to meet right after church on Sunday.

She was wondering how soon she could leave when he came over to her. "I am begging for a ride," he told her casually, facing her. "My truck is in the shop and I don't want to take a cab back."

"Of course," she forced the words out of her mouth.

"Thanks," he told her briefly, striding away to collect some papers he had on a desk. She waited outside for him while he closed up.

She got in the car as soon as she saw him coming and he got into the passenger side.

He tried to adjust his long frame to the bucket seat, shifting several times until he got comfortable. "I missed you at church the week before," he commented.

"I was not feeling well," she shrugged, her eyes on the road.

"So Deacon said," he was staring at her and she felt his eyes on her. "Were you really not feeling well?"

She sent him a heated look, turning back to the road as she saw the hint of amusement on his face.

"I don't have to answer to you," she said loftily; praying that she would reach his house quickly. It was a cool night and she had forgotten to wear a sweater. She wound up the window with a slight shiver.

"Cold?" his voice was concerned. And before she knew what he was doing, she felt his hand on her arm; slowly rubbing it.

"What are you doing?" she asked sharply, pulling away from him.

"Trying to warm you up," he drawled. "Or am I making you too hot?"

"You wish," she retorted, her skin still tingling from his touch.

With a sigh of relief she saw that they had reached his house and she slowed down and came to a stop; expecting him to get out.

"Want some coffee?" he queried, not moving.

"No thanks, I really need to get home," she told him, not looking at him. She did not trust herself to be alone with him.

"Please?" he said softly. "Besides I want to show you my house."

With a sigh Sara capitulated.

The house was three bedrooms and a big living room with comfortable furniture; there was a keyboard and a piano that stood proudly in the corner of the room. She caught a glimpse of a dining room with a large table and several chairs. "Too big for one person, I know," he said wryly as he came back with the cups of coffee. "Still take it black?"

She nodded. She had sat down on a small red couch, to discourage him from sitting beside her but to her consternation; he pulled up a chair and sat in front of her, crowding her.

"Were you seeing someone?" he asked her abruptly, placing his cup on a table beside them.

"What?" she asked him startled.

"Were you seeing anyone while you were away Sara," he repeated impatiently.

"That's none of your business," she told him heatedly, putting down her cup with the intention of leaving; but he wouldn't let her.

"I kept thinking about you with someone else," he told her grimly. "And I wanted to die."

"You were with someone as well," she whispered, her heart aching at the tortured expression on his face.

"I tried," he stared at her. "I convinced myself that if I tried hard enough I could replace you with her. She is a nice girl, a girl any man would be proud to call his own but she was not you and every time I kissed her, I saw your face and eventually she realized and she told me that I was not ready for a relationship with someone else. She loved me and I could not love her back, because of you."

Sara did not know what to say; she wished he had not told her but secretly she was glad that he had not been able to be with someone else. "I'm sorry," she mumbled.

"That's such an inadequate word isn't it?" he mused. "Sorry I ruined your life, sorry I destroyed the love I gave you, sorry I stamped all over your heart. So inadequate."

"David," she began huskily, reaching out a hand to touch his strong jaw.

"Don't," he groaned and without another word he pulled her into his arms onto his lap. "I have tried so hard to forget you but I can't" he whispered; his head coming down towards her; hovering as if waiting for her to stop him but she could not; she did not want to and with a sigh she reached up and put her hands around his neck. "Sara," he groaned, taking her lips with his.

Sara's mouth opened and she welcomed his kisses, her arms tightening around his neck as his tongue delved inside her mouth. One hand reached inside her blouse and brushed against the silk of her bra; touching the hardened nipple. She shuddered with need and her body quaked as he ran his finger over her nipple, his mouth moving over hers hungrily.

Sara wanted more. He was driving her crazy with need and she wanted to feel him inside her.

"David," she tore her lips away from his. "Please."

His mouth grazed her cheek and went further until he took the nipple inside his mouth, stroking it lovingly. Sara cried out, gripping his hair tightly, arching her back against his onslaught; she was lost and almost begging him to take her.

Suddenly, he released her nipple and set her back on the couch. Sara stared at him, her body quivering with unfulfilled need.

"I can't" he told her huskily, he had stood up and had started pacing; his expression tortured. "I can't get over what you did and I suffered too much when you left."

Trembling, Sara buttoned up her blouse, her expression one of mortification. She had almost begged him to make love to her. She stood up resolutely, passing a hand over her slightly mussed hair. "I understand," she told him coolly; there was no way she was going to let him see how much she was suffering and he was right; she had hurt him so much in the past; how could she expect him to forgive her now?

"Do you?" he looked at her with narrowed eyes. She looked so unbelievably sexy; with her slumberous dark brown eyes with their golden tints and her nipples evident in the thin blouse; it was taking all of his will not to drag her back into his arms and take her right there on the floor.

"Yes, I do," she turned and headed towards the door.

"This is not finished Sara," he warned her huskily as her hand reached for the door knob. "Not by a long shot." She hesitated briefly then twisted the knob and went outside without a word.

Sara drove home blindly, her thoughts crowding inside her head. She had thought she was over him; she had thought she was in love with Michael but realize now that it was just a surface emotion; nothing like what she felt for David. She had wanted so much for him to make love to her and she shivered as she remembered how his lips felt on hers – she had almost abandoned her pride and beg him to take her.

She reached home and parked the car, sitting there silently – she had turned off the radio; she needed time to think and regroup. She had spent so much time running away from her emotions that they were at last catching up to her.

Michael had told her one time that she was too cool and uptight and she needs to loosen up. With David, she had always been herself; he knew who she was and what she was about.

Sara bit her lip as she remembered the first time they had made love. It had been the first time for both of them and she smiled sadly as she recalled how gentle he had been. They had sneaked into his house when his parents had gone to church that night. It had been her eighteenth birthday and they had wanted to celebrate it together. He had stolen a bottle of wine and taken it up to his room and had bought her a cupcake with a candle in it. They had started kissing, then he had taken off her clothes, his hands trembling. He had told her how beautiful she was, the most beautiful woman he had ever seen in his life and he wanted to please her so much. She had taken off his clothes shyly; her innocent hands reaching out to take hold of his penis; her expression curious. They had fumbled their way around each other and when he placed his erection inside her she had cried out in pain. He had wanted to stop but she would not let him and after a while the pain had lessened and the pleasure had increased. He came before her; his hoarse cry echoing around the room; she came soon after; sinking her teeth into his shoulder as the pleasure coursed through her body. It had taken a while for his shoulder to heal and the bite marks to fade and he wore it proudly; saying it was her brand on him.

Sara stared unseeingly into the night. The night had gone a little chilly and she shivered slightly; it was such a beautiful night and summers always brought back such bitter sweet memories. So much had happened to her over the past years and she just wanted to settle down and sort her life out. She had thought she could cut it as a model but she had done a short stint and she had not made it – and the glossiness and shallow living had lost its appeal as far as she was concerned.

Sara got out of the car and locked the doors; making sure the alarm was activated and then she went inside. Her father was still up and with a cheerful smile, she greeted him. He was sitting in his favorite rocker by the window and reading his Bible. "Everything went well?" he placed his finger on the page as he looked at her.

"Yes," she told him, going over to kiss his cheek softly. "I am going to bed now Dad, don't stay up too late."

She went up to her bedroom and took off her clothes going straight to the bathroom; and it was there with the water running off her body that she gave in to her emotions; her body shaking with tears.

Chapter 4

"Pass me the lemon juice will you? It's in the refrigerator on the top shelf," Callie stirred the chicken and covered it to simmer. Sara passed the lemon juice to her. They were at Callie's house and she was busy preparing dinner for her men, as she called them. She had invited Sara over for dinner and her husband and son had gone to the park for the afternoon.

"I can't get over how domesticated you have become," Sara marveled, taking a seat on the stool by the counter and propping her chin on her hand as she watched her friend move around the kitchen. The house was nice and homely, with touches of color everywhere and scattering of toys all around. Callie had given up working at an accounting firm to be a stay at home mom.

"That's me I have become a stepford wife and the kind of woman we used to deride, remember?" she shook her head wryly. It was Saturday afternoon and a week had passed since the debacle at David's house and Sara was almost back to normal. She had seen him one time after that when they had met with the young people to plan some more but he had kept his distance and so had she.

"Do you have any regrets?" Sara popped a grape into her mouth and chewed the sweet fruit with relish. She was still in her work clothes; jeans and a dress shirt and her father had shooed her out to go and do something; so she had accepted Callie's invitation.

"About marrying Paul or staying at home?" Callie's eyebrows rose inquiringly as she sprinkled lemon juice into the pot with the chicken.

"Staying at home," Sara said.

"Sometimes," Callie shrugged, coming to sit on the stool beside Sara. "Sometimes I feel like I would just tear my hair out. And when Ben is asleep, I find myself wandering the house trying to find something to do; there is only so much daytime T.V. you can watch before you start growing numb."

"I don't know if I could do it," Sara said reflectively. "Does that make me sound selfish?"

"You're who you are girl," Callie went to turn the knob on the stove. Then she went to the fridge and poured them both a refreshing glass of iced tea. "I had a miscarriage two years ago, and my marriage have not been the same ever since."

"Oh Callie, I am so sorry," Sara exclaimed, putting down her drink and placing a hand on her friend's.

"Paul and I went through a pretty rough patch and we separated for a couple of months," she shook her head. "For a long time we were not sure we would ever be okay again but we're getting there by the help of God." She turned and faced Sara. "I needed you there and you weren't. You were my best friend and I couldn't even call you; I went through hell Sara and I did not have my best friend around to help me get through it."

Sara felt the shame wash over her. She had disappointed so many people that she wondered if she was ever going to make up for what she did. She had given in to her selfish ambitions and had not cared one bit who she hurt in the process. "I was younger and very foolish and I wanted to spread my wings and I was not about to let anyone stop me.

Not a loved one; not my best friend," she look at Callie soberly.

Callie shook her head and got up; coming over to the devastated girl and giving her a hug. "You should have trust me enough to tell me what was going on with you," she told her fiercely. "I probably would have tried to talk you out of it but I would have listened."

"I know," Sara said tearfully, returning her hug gratefully. "Oh Callie, I have made such a mess of things and I don't know how to fix it."

"Stop trying to fix it," Callie told her; giving her a squeeze before letting go and going over to the stove to save the rice that was simmering on low fire. "It will sort itself out and David will come around," she looked at her friend shrewdly.

"How did you know-?" Sara stopped in mid-sentence.

"How did I know you two still love each other?" Callie looked at her mildly. "The sparks fly when you're near girl; you two belong together."

"I am not sure he thinks that anymore," Sara said miserably.

"He will, if he doesn't already," Callie advised. Just then they heard Paul and Benjamin's chatter coming up the driveway. "Men like to be pushed in the right direction." She added; turning around to catch the running Benjamin as he launched himself into her arms chattering a mile a minute.

They had dinner and Sara felt better than she had since she had gotten back. Callie was her best friend again and she felt as if she was actually getting somewhere.

*****

The concert was well on its way and the performances were well appreciated by the audience. The church hall was packed to capacity and Sara was backstage with Callie and David and several others who were helping with props and costume changes. She had chosen to wear a flowing pink and green summer dress that left her arms bare and big gold earrings and matching bracelets. She had on minimum make up and she had caught David looking at her several times, but she had ignored him. Callie was right; it will sort itself out.

He performed a solo himself and when it was time for him to go out; he glanced at her briefly and then left.

"I told you," Callie whispered with a grin. Paul and Benjamin were seated in the second row so that she could keep an eye on them. "That man is into you."

Sara ignored her and wandered to the side of the stage, to take a peek at him. His singing had improved and he held his audience captive with a song he had composed; entitled: 'God's Grace is Bigger'. She found herself clapping enthusiastically as he finished, among cries of 'encore' but he graciously declined and made way for the next act.

The concert was finished at ten and Sara wished it had continued – she had enjoyed herself immensely. Her father was long gone, claiming extreme weariness and Callie had to rush home because Ben was coming down with something. "Call me tomorrow," she told Sara as she rushed out.

Sara stayed behind to help with the cleaning up and so did David. Before long, everyone had trickled out leaving them both. She helped him lock up and they went out to the parking lot. It was almost eleven o'clock but Sara felt energized and not in the least bit sleepy.

"Had fun?" he asked her as they walked to her car. His truck was parked next to hers.

"Tremendously," she laughed gaily. She had brought a thin sweater which she put on over her dress; it was starting to feel a little chilly.

"I'm glad," he said softly.

She made to open her car door and then stopped, turning to face him. "You have a wonderful talent, David," she told him sincerely.

"Thanks," he murmured. He was standing in front of her and Sara found herself wondering what he would do if she just leaned into him and kissed him. Without even thinking about it she got closer to him and put her arms around his neck. "Sara?" his voice was husky.

"I want to kiss you," she told him and before he could respond she stood on her toes to reach his mouth. He smelled of his familiar elusive cologne and the cool night air and as his breath stirred her face she moaned; her tongue delving inside his mouth. For a moment, he stood rigid and then with a muffled groan he pulled her closer to him and returned the kiss with ardor. He bore back against the car, one hand reaching to touch her unfettered breasts; rubbing against the nipple while his mouth ravished hers. Sara sagged against the car; she was trembling; her heart thundering inside her chest. She had to have him and it had to be now.

It was the glare of headlights that brought them back to where they were. "Not here," he muttered harshly, wrenching his lips from hers. He rested his forehead against hers, trying to bring his breathing under control.

"I need you," she told him huskily.

He groaned and his hands tightened around her. "Come home with me," he breathed.

"It's too late," she said helplessly, her body vibrating. "I didn't say anything to my Dad."

"Have dinner with me tomorrow at my place," he sighed against her lips.

She nodded, her heart thundering. She lifted her head and gazed at him; his breath caught in his throat as he stared at her face, illuminated by the street light. Her coffee and cream complexion was flushed with excitement and her eyes were heavy lidded. She looked like sex, there was no better way to put it and he felt the heaviness in his loins. He needed her desperately.

"You have to leave now," he told her hoarsely, his eyes holding hers. "I can't hold out if you don't go." With a groan, he took her lips with his roughly; his hands crushing her and then letting go abruptly, striding away to wrench open the door of his truck and going inside.

He watched her until she had driven out of the parking lot and then he followed behind her to make sure she had reached home safely.

She could not sleep that night and she found herself twisting and turning; going over and over in her mind what they had done and how his touch had made her feel. She had wanted so much to go home with him, she wanted him so much. She finally fell asleep in the wee hours of the morning but it was a sleep that was sprinkled with confusing dreams about David.

*****

She had told her father she was going out to dinner and he had given her a quizzical look before he nodded. "See you when I see you," he told her with a slight smile. The store had not been busy and she had left a little after five. David had told her to come over as soon as she was finished at the store. She got to his house half an hour later and just sat in the car, wondering what on earth she was doing. She had dressed carefully in a tan pantsuit, cream blouse and tan heels. She had gold hoops at her ears and a thin gold chain around her neck.

"Are you going to sit out there all evening?" his voice jolted her out of her reverie and Sara jumped guiltily. She had been so deep in thought that she had not heard him approaching. He was leaning against the gate and his expression was amused. He was in jeans and a white T-shirt and his hair was slightly tousled by the breeze.

"I was just getting out," she told him defensively, climbing out of the car.

"And here I was thinking maybe you were getting cold feet." He teased, opening the gate to let her in. He was so close that her breast brushed against his chest, causing her to jump slightly. She was jumpy and nervous and she was annoyed with herself.

"Why would you think that?" she brushed past him, not seeing the admiring look he gave her.

"Make yourself at home," he told her heading for the kitchen. "I have iced tea, root beer and lemonade in the fridge, drink something."

Sara had taken off her shoes and was in her stocking feet. She wandered over to the large double sided fridge and took a glass from the sideboard and poured herself some lemonade. She caught a glimpse of him inside the kitchen, busily stirring something on the stove. "This was your aunt's house wasn't it?" she asked him; she had wandered into the kitchen and perched on a stool at the counter.

"Yes," he nodded. "She left it to me and I did some renovations; still doing some. I have some ideas – I am planning to build a gazebo and wraparound benches in the garden and a green grocery around the side."

"That sounds like a good idea and something the neighborhood needs," Sara said approvingly, sipping her ice cold drink.

"Thanks," he told her. "Ready to eat?"

"What's for dinner?" she asked him, sniffing the air.

"My famous chicken pot pie and apple tart. Do you mind if we eat in here?"

"I would love that," she told him.

He put the place mats on the counter and asked her to get some plates from the cupboard. The meal was delicious and Sara found herself asking for more. "When did you learn to cook so well?" she asked him curiously, she was on her second helping of apple tart.

"Mom taught me the basics and I love to experiment," he reached over and used a finger to wipe sauce from her chin, bringing the finger to his mouth to lick it.

Don't make it sexual, she told herself firmly as she stared at him.

"Finished?" he asked her, getting up to put the dishes inside the sink.

She nodded not trusting herself to speak.

"Want any coffee?" he asked as she slid off the stool.

"No," she murmured. He had come up beside her and his hands trapped her against the counter. "David?" she leaned back against the counter.

"Hmm," he was busy. Looking at her slightly parted lips which still had the rose gloss she had put on shortly before she came over. Her eyes which were slightly lowered and heavy lidded. He was busy, fighting the feeling that threatened to overcome him. His mouth lowered slowly and Sara waited, not moving as he reached within a hairs breadth of her lips, his breath touching her. He took her lips with his and she succumbed; she had been waiting so long for this. She had anticipated how she would feel and what she would do but all of that fled through the window as his lips touched hers. His mouth was hard against hers and even though he was not touching anywhere else on her body; her entire being was flooded with warmth and she felt the tingling traveling from her toes upwards. It was she who did the touching, the reaching out as she twined her arms around his neck, pressing her body closer to him; willing him to hold her but he didn't, he continued to torture her with his mouth; his kisses taking her breath away; almost had her begging for more.

He broke the kiss and leaned his forehead against hers, his breathing harsh. They stayed that way for a time, neither of them saying anything – he was not holding her and she had her arms still around his neck. She was wondering what he was thinking and torturing herself on how she could make him see how sorry she was. "You always have a way of making me forget where I am and what I am about," he told her huskily; lifting his head. "Here we are in my kitchen and I can't wait to get you in my bed and tear off your clothes; what have you done to me Sara? What is this power you have over me that no matter how much you hurt me I can't hate you? I run straight back into your arms?"

"Let me go," Sara pushed against him but he would not budge. And as Sara looked up at him, she saw it; the confusion, the sadness and the passion, emotions he had no control over, emotions he was wrestling with. She felt the tenderness washed over her; tenderness for this man who had been broken when she had left and she wanted to ease his pain and tell him she was here and never leaving again; but he would not believe her; words would not do it now, maybe action would.

"I hate myself for hurting you so much," she told him softly, reaching a hand to touch his rigid jaw, roughened by an overnight growth. He was always saying that no matter how often he shaved, he just could not keep up with the growth of hair on his face. "I wish I could take it back but I cannot and I don't know what to do,"

He stood there looking down at her, his expression not changing. Then with a tortured groan he closed his arms with stunning force. His lips came down and his mouth moved over hers with bruising force; opening up a maelstrom that swept them along with a force that swept them away on its tide.

Sara held on to him; her body moving restlessly against his; her arms tight around his neck. With a swift movement, he swept her off her feet and into his arms, never once breaking the kiss; his mouth moving hers desperately as if he broke the contact she would leave.

Chapter 5

Sara barely caught a glimpse of a large minimalist bedroom before he placed her on his king sized gently. "I want to undress you slowly and see every inch of your body," he murmured. "I want to take my time but I don't know if I can."

Her blouse buttoned at the front and he slowly pulled the first one open. It was pure torture for her as she lie still; letting him do what he wanted. He finally pulled the shirt from the waistband of her pants. Then he just looked at her; one hand trailing over the generous curve of her breast over the lace of her white bra.

"You're so beautiful," he pushed away the scrap of material; exposing her full round flesh with nipples as hard as pebbles. "I used to dream about you; about doing this to you and wondered if I would ever get the chance again," He bent his head and Sara arched her body in anticipation of his mouth on her. He sucked her nipple inside his mouth; pulling on it and blowing, causing the tension to build up inside her. She sank her fingers in his hair; a cry building up inside her throat. He shifted to her other breast to give it the same attention.

He sat up and kneeled over her, pulling down her pants to reveal tiny matching panties. His fingers trailed over her upper thigh, dangerously close to her pubic area. His head was bent as he looked at her. Sara came up on her elbows so that she could get a better look at him. There was no light in the bedroom; only the sliver of light in the passage way. His hair had fallen down on his forehead and Sara wanted to brush it back. He took off her panties and then took off his clothes. Sara stared at him; her heart jumping inside her chest. He had filled out. He was not the same lanky boy from her childhood days, the muscles rippled on his chest and arms and there was a sprinkling of dark hair drifting down to his pubic area. His erection stood out proudly and she remembered how she had always teased him that maybe he was part black because how else would he be so generously endowed.

He watched her watching him and he watched as she reached out and touch him there, causing a jolt to enter his body. He ran his hand over her pubic area, fingers drifting down to her opening which was already wet. She opened her legs to him and he dipped his fingers inside her; watching her face as he worked his fingers inside. Sara clamped her legs tight around his fingers, her back arching. "David," she cried out, her hands gripping the sheets.

"Tell me what you want me to do," he said hoarsely, his fingers pressing inside her. "Tell me what to do to you."

"I want you inside me please," She gasped. "Please David, I want you inside me."

He took out his fingers, moist with her wetness and rose over her, guiding his erection inside her; she opened up for him and he eased inside her tightness, his teeth clenched. He started moving and she went with him; lifting her hips to draw him in closer. "Sara!" he cried out hoarsely, taking her lips with his as he plunged inside her, his hands tight on her hips as he lifted her to meet his thrusts. She closed over him like a vice and met his thrusts with her frenzied ones. She had missed this and she did not realized it; she had missed him and the way he made her feel and she had been contented to live with second best. He filled her up and she fitted him so well that it was like they were molded together as one.

She lifted her legs and clasped them around his waist, giving him more, wanting more of him. He came before her, he wanted to wait for her but he could not hold back any longer and releasing her mouth he cried out hoarsely as he spilled his seed inside her; his body shaking. His spasms were over before she started feeling the sensation rushing through her. "David," she cried out, digging her fingers into his shoulders as the wave crashed over her. He held her to him as they both rode out the wave together.

He rested his forehead against hers and she held him to her; loathe letting him go. There was so much she wanted to say to him; how sorry she was and how she would never make the mistake of leaving again if he only gave her a second chance.

But before she could say anything; he rolled off and got off the bed leaving her cold and lonely without his body on hers. "It's late, and your dad may be wondering where you are," he told her abruptly, pulling on his pants.

Sara stiffened and with a resolute look on her face she slid off the bed; looking for pieces of her clothing. To hell with him, she thought as she hurriedly got dressed. His back was to her and he had sat on a flimsy piece of ottoman that looked out of place in the room.

"I'm ready," she told him stiffly; already going towards the door.

He caught her just as she reached the hallway and pulled her arm to turn her around. "I want to beg you to stay with me and forget the hurt and pain I felt when you left; I want to bury myself inside you over and over again but I can't, not now." He told her roughly and with a groan he took her lips in a bruising kiss that had her leaning against him weakly; then he released her; his breathing irregular.

"Go Sara," he told he wearily. "Please, before I change my mind." She left without a word and when she got into her car she saw him at the window looking out at her. She gunned the engine and drove off; combing a hand through her tousled hair; her mind in turmoil and her body craving him.

*****

He didn't call her. Not even to find out if she had reached home safely. Sara told herself she did not care; but she did and that night she found herself going over the night and her body tingled as she remembered what it had been like. She loved him and she knew that now; but the problem was how was she going to convince him she was here to stay and she was not going anywhere?

The next day at work she hardly had time to think about him; the store was so busy. It was summer break and the children and young people had decided to spend some time at the bookstore; probably to get out of the stifling heat or to take advantage of the free Wi-Fi services offered. Some of them even bought books and CDs. Her father had stepped out for a bit and she was manning the store by herself. It was approaching three o'clock and the store had emptied somewhat when she came in. Sally Graham was a female replica of her son; she only lacked his towering height and Sara remembered the many times she had been at her house when she and David were together. Sara felt herself standing to her full height unconsciously as she turned to face the petite woman; she'd seen her at church the times she had been there but had always managed to avoid her.

"My dear," she greeted Sara warmly. "I have not officially seen you since your return."

Sara forced a smile and greeted the older woman, taking her small hand in hers. "Hi Sally, you haven't aged a bit."

"And you have done something wonderful with your hair," Sally walked over and sat on one of the chairs available, forcing Sara to do the same. "You are such a beautiful girl; I can see why my David is finding it hard to get over you."

"Sally, I am sorry but my relationship with David is not up for discussion," Sara said firmly even though she was quaking inside. The woman hated her and she could not blame her.

"So there is a relationship?" she looked at the girl curiously. She was so beautiful and David did not stand a chance.

"That's between us," Sara said politely, wishing a ton of customers would invade the store to save her from this awkward conversation.

"When you left David several years ago, I had to pry him out of bed." She began as if she did not hear her. "He would not eat and he spent his nights just staring at the phone hoping it would ring and hoping it would be you. I ached for him and I found myself wishing I could give him something to ease his pain; but it's not like a physical pain is it? You can't just give a person a pill and say take two times a day for a week, can you? So I sat there watching him suffer and could not do anything about it and now you're back, looking more beautiful than ever and my David is back to suffering again; only this time it is even worse because he gets to see you and remember and want and wonder if he allows you back in; if you'll leave again."

Sara sat there and listened to every word that dug spikes inside her heart and she did not know what to say but she refused to apologize to David's mother – she was not David.

"I can't take back what I did," Sara told her soberly. "But I am telling you right now that it's between David and I."

Sally sat there measuring the younger girl coolly, her hazel eyes considering. Sara had worn a simple cotton dress with thin straps and she looked young and vibrant. Her make-up was light and almost colorless lip gloss highlighted her full lips.

"I wish he was twelve years old again so that I could forbid him to see you," she said with a slight smile. "But I can't, can I? He is a grown man and I can't tell him what to do and who to see. He will do what he pleases; all I can do is pray for him."

"I am sure that is enough," Sara told her calmly. The woman was all but telling her that she was praying for her not to be a part of David's life and she felt as if she was barely holding on. David still had not called her and now his mother was here castigating her, it was too much. "I think you underestimate

David, he can take care of himself just fine. And he is not running back into my arms like you think. Like I said; you underestimate him."

"I don't hate you," Sally stood, staring at her. "It would be unchristian for me to do so, I just hate what you did to my son and one day when you grow up and have children you will find out."

"I am grown up," Sara's voice was frosty. "And I understand. Some mothers do not like to see their children hurt."

"I am sorry about your mother my dear," Sally told her. "Truly I am, but my first priority is to David and I make no apologies for that." With that she turned around and left, leaving Sara sitting there fighting back tears. It was when several customers came in that she got up and with a determined smile she went and do her job; she was not about to let anyone get her down; least of all David's mother.

*****

David balled up the paper and threw it towards the waste basket and it missed yet again. The room was strewn with paper he had discarded in his attempt to write the commentary he was supposed to be writing. He was a freelance editor for the local newspaper and had started out doing one article a week to now being asked to do four articles for the week. It was something he did aside from his work in the greenhouse and if people asked him which he preferred; he would have no idea what to tell them. But right now he was having a hard time thinking. He had not slept the night before; and her scent was all over his bed, so much so that he had changed the sheets; but putting on fresh ones did not help because her scent still lingered in his room. He should not have taken her to bed. But what else could he have done? He had thought making love with her would probably get her out of his system but that had backfired on him; what it had done was to make her dig deeper inside him and now he wanted to see her so bad he was trembling from it.

"Damn you Sara," he whispered brokenly; burying his head in his hands. He had spent so many years trying to get over her and when he had finally reached a place where he could go on without her; she had come back looking more achingly beautiful than before. He had not done an ounce of work since he had been up at dawn. His green house needed his attention and his article was due tomorrow.

He stood up and went to the window to look out on his garden. It was a very hot day and the sun was blazing down on his begonias and petunias making them look wilted. He had found out from an early age that he loved to dig in the dirt and he loved to plant things. When other boys his age were playing with action figures and riding bikes, he was making a garden at the back of his parents' house. His dad had bought him a trowel and some seeds and had told him that if he did not pay attention to plants, they end up dying. He had made sure they didn't.

With a sigh, he turned away from the window and went to the kitchen, maybe sustenance was what he needed but he knew what he wanted right now was Sara underneath him and him inside her. He closed his eyes as he remembered every smell and nuance of her body and how he felt inside her and his groan was potent as he felt himself hardening with desire. She was in his blood and there was no way she was getting out; he just did not know what to do about it.

*****

"Girl what did you expect?" Callie stirred sugar in her tea and look at Sara curiously. "You broke her only child's heart and now you're back and it's not as if he has moved on from you; he's still in hook, line and sinker."

"Thanks," Sara said dryly. They had met for lunch at the restaurant close to the bookstore and she was telling Callie of her encounter with Sally Graham yesterday at the store. "And he's not into me hook, line and sinker."

Callie looked at her wryly as she sipped her herbal tea. "I have a son and I would tear out a woman's hair if he hurt my son."

"You're making me feel real good right about now," Sara bit into her burger with relish.

"I live to please," Callie grinned impishly. "Honey, cut her some slack. She still thinks of David as her baby and that's not going to end anytime soon. So are you guys are back together?"

"No we're not!" Sara said hastily; causing Callie to raise her brows.

"You're protesting too much honey," Callie told her dryly.

"He has not called me since," Sara shrugged carelessly. "And I don't care."

"Since what?"

"Since we were with each other on Sunday night," Sara told her avoiding her gaze.

"Ah," Callie murmured. "No wonder 'Mommy' is protective; she probably knows or if she doesn't, she is there thinking that it's only a matter of time. Give him time Sara; he probably hates the fact that he's so weak when it comes to you."

"I am not going to hurt him again Callie," Sara said with determination. "I am not that person anymore."

"It's not me that needs convincing girl," Callie told her shrewdly. "It's David."

They ate the rest of the meal in relative silence with Callie filling her in on some of the escapades of Benjamin. She went back to the store thoughtfully. She had not told her father of her encounter with Sally Graham and had no intention of doing so; the less people knew the better.

*****

Sara did not see David until Wednesday night at church when they had Bible study and she was careful to sit as far away from him as possible. He had not called her and she had made up her mind not to call him either. She was not going to risk getting rejected. Her father had stayed at the store to do some stocktaking and had urged her to go.

When Bible study was finished, she hurried out to the parking lot. She had to get out of there before he came out. But as she opened her door she heard his voice behind her. "Running away?" he drawled. Sara closed her eyes briefly and slowly turned around to face him. He looked so damned good and she ached for him.

"I need to get home, I have something to do." She told him stiffly.

"I am sure you do," he smiled wryly, shoving his hands into the pockets of his black dress pants. His yellow shirt was unbuttoned at the top and she saw just a glimpse of his chest hair.

"I have to leave," she told him abruptly, turning around to enter her car.

"I wanted to call you," he told her huskily; his voice stopping her. "I did not know what to say to you or what to do about what I am feeling Sara. I am constantly thinking about you and I don't know what to do, I needed some space."

"You got it," her back was still turned towards him and she stiffened when she felt his touch on her shoulder.

"I am up and down when it comes to you Sara," he told her wearily. He turned her around to face him. There was a slight breeze and it stirred the hair on her forehead. He pushed it away gently and Sara quivered. "I kid myself that I was over you and I had moved on," he gave a self-deprecating smile. "But I am not and I don't know what to do about it; about you."

"Your mother seems to think I am going to be the death of you," she told him; her expression sober.

"My mother?" he stared at her puzzled. "What does she have to do with us?"

"She came to the store and told me what she thought of me." Sara said grimly.

"Oh Jesus," David muttered, running fingers through his hair. "What did you say to her?"

"I just told her that it's between us," Sara shrugged. "But I am sure she does not have anything to worry about, does she David?"

"What do you mean by that?" he asked her, his gaze narrowing.

"It means that you don't want to have anything to do with me." She told him heatedly. "It means that you probably think I am going to hurt you again and you would not want to make the same mistake twice."

"Sara stop it," he told her harshly. "Can you blame me for being cautious?" He gripped her arms; exercising restraint as he saw that there were several members coming outside. "I can't do this here," he muttered releasing her. "Come home with me."

"No," Sara said firmly, pulling her door open. "I am giving you time and space." She got in and slammed her door shut, putting the car in reverse and driving away without waiting for his response.

When she got home she switched off the car and sat there. She could not face her father yet and she knew he was waiting up for her; she needed time to think. She closed her eyes and leaned back against the headrest.

She remembered a particularly difficult time in her teen years when she had told her father she did not want to go to school and she wished she could stay home. He had told her that staying away from school was not an option and whatever it was that was bothering her she should discuss it with him and he would try to work it out. That morning she had slammed out of the house and had told him that she hated him and she wished it was him who had gone and not her mom. She had refused to feel guilty about the painful look on his face and had gone off to school in a huff; mad with the world.

She had been sitting outside on one of the school benches during lunch; Callie had gone off in search of Kevin; her current boyfriend so she had sat there just brooding. "What's wrong?" he'd came and sat beside her, tucking in his long, lanky legs under the bench.

"What makes you think something is wrong?" she had asked him coolly, lifting her pointed chin as she looked at him.

"Because you look like you're about to explode and you're sitting out here all by yourself," he pointed out; a lock of hair falling down on his forehead, giving him an endearing look. He was fifteen and she was fourteen and even though they went to the same church; she had never spared him more than a passing glance. She had no interest in boys at that time.

She had shrugged and looked away; her interest caught by a boy and a girl in a passionate embrace.

"Your mother leaving was not your fault," he told her quietly causing Sara's head to whip around sharply, her eyes blazing as she stared at him.

"How dare you talk about my mother? It's none of your damn business," Her voice had gone hoarse as she fought back tears.

"It's okay to cry," he had told her, completely unfazed by her outburst. And Sara had cried. She remembered him pulling her into his arms and rubbing her back soothingly until she was spent. She had tried to pull away when she was done but he wouldn't let her and she had stayed that way for a while before she pulled away.

"Feeling better?" he had asked her, not in the least bit embarrassed that a girl had cried buckets on his shoulder.

She had nodded and used the back of her hands to wipe her wet cheeks. And then she had told him what she had said to her father. He had told her to go home and apologize and explain what she was feeling and he was sure her father would understand and forgive her.

She had done just that and her father had told her gently that there was nothing she could ever do or say to him for him to hate her.

She and David had become friends from then and later in years had become a couple. He had always been there for her and she had taken him for granted and broke his heart because she had thought about only herself. His mother was right; it was up to her to prove to him that she would never do that to him. If time was what he needed; she would give him that; even though it killed her to be away from him.

Chapter 6

She was ill. She had woken up Friday morning with a raging headache and an itchy throat and she was running a temperature. It was five o'clock in the morning and she hated to wake her father; besides she felt too weak to even get off the bed.

She scrambled off and went to the bathroom to get a glass of water to wet her parched throat. She was so dizzy she had to hold on to the counter. She never got sick, she thought irritably and because of that she didn't have even an aspirin in the bathroom cupboard. She dug around and found some Nyquil which she swallowed with slight distaste.

It took her a little while to get back into her bedroom and into bed. By that time she was washed with sweat. She settled back against her pillows with a sigh of relief and went straight back to sleep.

It was when her father called her name several times that she woke up with a start." Honey are you ill?" he asked in concern, using the back of his hand to rest on her forehead. "Darling you are burning up!" he exclaimed.

"I'm sorry dad," she told him miserably. "I feel awful."

"I am going to get you some tea and a cold rag for your face," he told her, leaving the room hurriedly.

Sara sank back on the pillow, her energy spent. He came back into the room shortly after with a tray of tea and a slice of plain toast and a glass of water. He put the tray on the bed and eased her up against the pillow and set the tray on her lap. "I want you to try and eat this and drink the liquid, your body needs it and I am going to bring up a bottle of orange juice for you to drink as well. You need the vitamin C. Don't worry about the store, I'll manage." He made her promise to get some rest; then he left.

Sara nibbled on a piece of bread and drank down the tea and water; quenching her parched throat before putting the tray on the side table. She slept and woke up feeling a little better; at least she was not feeling as weak as before. "Glad to see that you are still in the land of the living." The soft voice beside her bed, almost had her screaming. What on earth was he doing here?

Her hand automatically went up to her hair which must be a sight.

"You could never look anything less than beautiful even if you tried," David said dryly, leaning over to put a hand on her forehead. It was as if he had scalded her; his touch affected her more than the fever had.

"What are you doing here?" she croaked.

"I went to the store to see you and your father told me you were holed up in bed with the flu." He told her. He was sitting on the side of her bed and was the epitome of good health, with his tanned skin, glowing with perfection and he smelled enticingly of sun and plants.

"You didn't have to come," she told him, her throat was parched again and her head felt dizzy.

"I didn't have to but I wanted to," he got up and poured some orange juice in a glass and handed it to her. Sara accepted it gratefully and downed the glass thirstily.

"I will be okay now so you don't have to stay," she handed the glass to him.

"I am not going anywhere," he told her mildly, kicking off his shoes and climbing into the bed; pulling her surprised body against his.

"David," she murmured halfheartedly, welcoming his warmth and solidness.

"Shh," he murmured, rubbing her back. "Go to sleep, I will be right here." She drifted off to sleep in his arms, her head on his chest. David held her to him with a tenderness that exposed his feelings and his heart constricting with the depths of it.

She woke up an hour later disoriented; not knowing where she was and it took her a minute to realize she was in David's arms. She lay there savoring his closeness and hoping fervently that she could stay that way forever.

"Feeling better?" his deep voice rumbled in his chest and vibrated against her face.
She shook her head yes; twisting to look up at him. He was staring down at her with a look that had her heart inside her throat. It was unbelievably tender.

"How about something substantial to eat?" he asked her lightly. "Hungry?"

"Starving," she told him hoarsely, her eyes locked with his; her meaning clear. He held her gaze for a moment then with a strangled groan he put her away from him; climbing out of bed.

"When I make love to you again Sara, it's not going to be when you're weak with a virus but when you're strong enough to match me move for move," he told her through clenched teeth before leaving her to go to the kitchen.

Sara sank back against the pillows, a gloating smile playing around her lips. Suddenly, being so ill was not too bad after all.

He had made her chicken soup and not the one from the can but chicken soup made with his own two hands and a slice of whole wheat bread. She took a sip and her eyes widened appreciatively. "This is good," she told him. He was sitting at the edge of the bed.

"Chicken soup for the physical being," he grinned teasingly.

"Your cooking skills have improved drastically," she told him with a shake of her head. She was indeed starving and she found herself drinking down the soup rapidly. He watched her until she finished eating and took the tray away from her. "How do you feel now?"

"As if I'm a new person," she told him gratefully. He came around, propped her pillow for her and she captured his hand. "Thank you," she whispered, bringing his hand to her lips.

"Sara," he groaned. "Don't please. I can't do this when you're in a weakened state and you're making it extremely difficult for me."

She placed an open mouth kiss in his palm and released his hand. He stood there looking at her, his eyes clouded over. "I'll behave," she told him impishly, settling back against the pillow.

He sent her a wry glance before sitting back on the edge of the bed.

"I am glad you came," she told him sincerely. She was starting to feel like her old self again and it was mostly due to him.

"I meant what I said the other night Sara," he leaned on his elbows and propped his feet on the bed, facing her. "Trying to stay away from you is like trying to stay away from myself," he gave a self-deprecating smile. "It's downright impossible."

"You don't trust me, I get it," she raised a hand as he started to protest. "I don't blame you David; I would do the same in your shoes. I told myself I was right to be angry at you at your mother for making me feel rotten but I did it to myself and I don't really deserve your forgiveness but I want to try and earn back your trust if you'll let me."

He stared at her, not knowing what to make of it. Here he was in her bedroom; in her bed and as much as he wanted to sink himself deep inside her, he had to practice constraint because of how weak she was. When her father had told him she was not feeling well he had wanted to drop everything and rush to her side but he had promised his father that he would pick something up at the store for him. He had chafed with impatience all the way and had almost killed himself getting here. He had watched her sleep and knew without a shadow of a doubt that it had to be her. It always had been her.

He looked away for a moment and his eyes caught a ratty teddy bear on a chair in the corner of the room. He remembered how she had always pretended to be tough but had kept the teddy bear he had won at the fair for her so many years ago. "You kept 'Bill'," he murmured softly. She had named him Bill the bear and had heatedly told him it was a good name for a stuffed toy.

"He got me through many lonely nights," she said softly.

"That day at the fair was one of my happiest memories of our relationship," he commented. "We ate so much popcorn and cotton candy that you accused me of trying to get you fat."

"And you got cotton candy all over my hair," she accused him with a laugh. They had spent the day holding hands and kissing when they were sure no grownups were looking. How innocent they had been then.

There was silence as they both drifted back in time; savoring the happy memories of their relationship and the time they had spent together.

"We can't get that back," he said abruptly, a frown creasing his forehead.

"We can't, but we can make others," she told him softly, holding his gaze. "We can make more lasting ones David; I am not the same girl I was before and I have no intention of leaving like I did before. I was naïve and scared and did not know what I wanted. I hurt the two most important people in my life and for that I am very sorry."

"What are you saying?" he asked her hoarsely.

"I want you back and if I have to make the first move then so be it. But this time I want it done officially; we go out on dates and we get to really know each other. I am asking for another chance David." She looked at him pleadingly.

He did not respond at once and Sara felt her heart sinking – if he said no she was not going to give up – surely he must still love her.

"I went out with several members from church because I wanted to see if there was any way I could move on from you," he said with a small smile. He was not looking at her and Sara wondered whether or not this was a good sign. "There was one whom I thought was going to be the one to help me move on but it didn't work out and I ended up doing to her what you did to me. I broke her heart and I have regretted it ever since. Thank God she has moved on since and is now married or I would still be flogging myself. I never stopped loving you

Sara," he looked at her; his eyes stormy. "I just did not like you but loving you have never been a problem."

"Do you think you can ever like me again?" she whispered.

"Oh Sara," he sighed; He slid closer to her and took her into his arms. "I just want to hold you right now and not think about anything else. May I do that?"

She nodded, closing her eyes as she rested against his broad shoulders with a contented sigh. It was a start.

When she woke up, he was gone and there was a note. With a hammering of her heart she reached for it, her hands trembling slightly.

"Darling Sara, I had to leave because just lying next to you was giving me ideas and I could not act on them. I would like us to start over and I want to start by saying that I never stopped loving you. I want you back in my life, I always have and always will but now I want you to do something for me: get better and we will have our date. I will be seeing you. I love you. David."

Sara held the letter to her; tears blurring her vision. He wanted her back and she knew she did not deserve to get him back but she was ecstatic. "Please God, I promise never to hurt him again and thank you for a second chance," she breathed a prayer. She wanted to call him but she held back; she had no intention of appearing desperate; no matter what she felt.

Her father came home that night and saw her up and about and in the kitchen putting the finishing touches on the dinner she had prepared. She had taken a much needed shower and had put on a T-shirt and sweat pants; she really did feel better.

"What are you doing up young lady," he asked scolding her.

"I'm fine Dad," she went over and kissed his cheek. "I made us dinner."

"I can see that," he looked at her shrewdly. "Any chance this change for the better had anything to do with young David's visit?" He pulled up a chair as she ladled chicken soup into a bowl. David had made plenty to serve for a meal and she had prepared a salad and baked a chocolate cake for dessert.

"Yes it does," she told him with a smile; as she sat down to join him. "He made me soup and I ate and we talked."

He sipped the soup and raised an eyebrow in surprised appreciation. "The young man can cook." He commented. "He loves you Sara, never stopped and when you went away he never stopped asking me for you."

"I have asked him for a second chance Dad," Sara told him.

Deacon Williams nodded. "We all deserve a second chance my dear and I am happy you are making amends and trying to make it work. You two belong together."

"Thanks Dad," she reached out a hand to grasp his. "I hurt you both so much and I can never make up for what I did."

"Loving someone means you forgive them over and over again my dear," he told her gently.

They ate the rest of the meal in silence and her father insisted on doing the washing up and urging her to go and get some rest. "You also have the day off tomorrow," he told her firmly.

"But Dad-" she started to protest.

"No buts girl. You need some more rest and maybe a chance to go somewhere. It's an order." He told her with a smile, turning back to the sink.

www.SaucyRomanceBooks.com/RomanceBooks

*****

Sara made the decision. She had called first to make sure they were going to be there. She had gotten the number from the personal directory in her father's office and she had not said anything to David. He had called her that night to find out how she was doing and had told her that he had some things to catch up on.

She knew the house well. She had been there so many times when she was younger. She had even been up in David's room where they had been on his bed just listening to music and chatting.

The place had not changed much since the four years she had been away. The garden had been a showpiece for quite some time and that still remained.

Sally greeted her at the door. Her striking resemblance to her son always amazed her. Her long dark hair was piled on top of her head to give her added height and she was wearing a cheerful apron over her summer dress.

"Come in dear, John is in the living room," she opened the door wider to let Sara pass her. They went into the room where David's father was seated on his favorite rocking chair.

He was a giant of a man with dark brown hair sprinkled liberally with gray and soft green eyes that always seemd to be smiling.

"My dear Sara, good to see you," he said in genuine delight as he rose and came over to give her a hug. She had always liked him because he went about with a cheerful smile and a pleasant countenance.

"Good to see you too John," Sara returned his hug.

Sally beckoned for her to take a seat and then she bustled out to get some lemonade and cookies. "So how have you been my dear?" John asked as soon as his wife went inside the kitchen. He had not been to church for the past few weeks because of a bad back so he had not seen her since she had been back.

"I am doing well thanks," she smiled at him.

"Your father must be pleased to have you back with him," he commented.

"He is," Sara nodded. Just then Sally came back with the refreshments and passed them out.

Sara took a sip of the ice cold lemonade and taking a deep breath, plunged right in. "I love David; I know you might not believe me but I really do love him." She stared down at the drink she had in her hand and missed seeing the looks exchanged by David's parents. "I messed up so much; I thought I wanted something more, something different and I was wrong. I left the love of a good man only to find out that there was not a better one than David. It took my leaving for me to realize that." She looked at Sally who was sitting there silent, allowing her to have her say. "You told me when I have children I would understand what seeing David like that did to you." John looked at his wife with a puzzled frown.

"My dear, you do not owe us an apology," he told her firmly. "What happened to David and you is between you too."

"I know that John but you are his parents and I am sure what I did affected both of you," Sara told him, she had replaced her glass on the table in front of her. "I am not apologizing; I am explaining because I want him back in my life and I want to clear the air."

"David has never loved anyone but you Sara," Sally smiled slightly. "He tried to kid himself that he was over you but he was not and I saw that. When I came to the bookstore the other day," she placed a calming hand on her husband's arm as he turned to look at her. "I was upset and it was not my place to upbraid you like that but being a mother I felt it was my duty to warn you not to hurt my son. He is an adult and he has to take care of himself."

"I know it's probably going to take a while before you accept me Sally but I am willing to wait," Sara told the woman earnestly. "I hope in time, we can be friends."

"My dear, I hope in time, we can be more than that," Sally said with a smile. "My son loves you no matter what happened and if he has forgiven you, who am I not to?"

Sara settled back against her chair, a smile of relief on her lips. She had crossed this hurdle; the only thing left now was to convince David that she was not going anywhere.

They had lunch and Sally took her into the garden to show her some prize roses she had planted. She spent the afternoon with David's parents and the feeling of discomfort and uncertainty she had felt when she came had slowly melted away.

She got home at a quarter to three and went to the kitchen to start preparing dinner. With a quiet resolution she went to work. The kitchen had her mother's stamp on it and she realized it was time to redecorate. She was not coming back and they need to move on. The first thing that had to go was the tablecloth that she had never liked in the first place; rummaging around in the linen closet she got out a plain linen tablecloth to replace it. Then she went to work taking down all the artwork that was on the wall and put up some murals she had acquired while she was away. With great satisfaction, she looked around the kitchen and living room and noticed the vast difference.

The phone rang just as she was about to make some dinner. It was David. "Hey you," his voice sent shivers down her spine.

"Hi," she said softly, sitting down on the stool and cradling the phone at her ear.

"I heard you went to see my parents," he teased. "Were you asking for my hand in marriage?"

"They told you," Sara said resigned. "Maybe I should have, would you have said yes?"

"Are you asking?"

"If you'll say yes I would," she told him seriously.

"Sara what are you doing to me?" he asked her hoarsely.

"Maybe the same thing you're doing to me," she told him huskily.

"I can't wait to see you," he muttered before hanging up. Sara sat there with the phone in her hand. She couldn't wait to see him either.

Chapter 7

He took her out to dinner. The restaurant was new and fancy and it had opened after she had left. She had dressed in an outfit courtesy of her modeling days; a rose colored satin dress flared at the waist and did not reach her knees. The shoulders were bare and made her slim neck appeared even longer. Her face was made up to perfection and looked flawless; she had on rose lip gloss. Gold earrings dangled at her lobes and she had on matching bangles.

"It always amazes me to see how beautiful you are," her father said with a shake of his head. It was Saturday night and he had come home and eaten and went straight to his comfortable chair in front of the television. He had noticed the changes she had made in the house and had nodded his head in approval.

"Thanks Dad," Sara gave him an air brush kiss.

"So I suppose I should not expect you home tonight?" he asked her gruffly, patting her bare arm.

"I don't think so," Sara said with a small uncomfortable smile.

"My dear, you have nothing to be embarrassed about; you're a grown woman and that man has been in love with you all his life," his eyes were twinkling.

"Thanks Dad, you're the best." She told him softly. She just knew he was going to fall asleep right in front of the television; like he always did.

Just then there was a knock on the door and for a minute she felt nervous; like a teenager out on her first date.

"Have a good time," Deacon Williams waved her away.

"Goodnight Dad, don't fall asleep in front of the T.V." she warned him.

He smiled at her and she went to open the door to admit David. He looked stunningly handsome in a dark blue jacket suit and light blue shirt with a red and blue striped tie. He stood there staring at her, his breath caught in his throat. "You take my breath away," he murmured throatily.

"Take care of my daughter David," her father called out from the hall.

"Always sir," he called back with a grin. Taking her arm he led her outside. A shiny black BMW was parked outside and Sara turned to look at him. "You have a car."

"I have a car," he told her teasingly, opening the passenger side for her to get in.

"With bucket seats as well," she murmured, running her hand over the seat.

"Mom shamed me into buying it," he admitted wryly, starting the car, the engine purring."She said one day I will be going on dates and no woman in their right mind will want to go out in the truck I use to transport fruits and vegetables in."

Sara laughed; leaning back against the headrest. "She was right."

"How are you?" he asked her softly, sending a quick glance her way.

"I am well on the way to recovery," she told him.

"I am glad," he told her; turning his concentration back on the road.

The restaurant had just a few people already seated and dining and they were shown to a corner booth and given menu cards.

Sara perused the menu and her eyes widened at the prices – even the simplest thing was expensive.

"Don't even think about it," he warned her; reading her expression correctly.

"What?" she asked defensively; putting aside her menu.

"Order what you want Sara, I can afford it," he told her dryly. "Don't worry, we won't be asked to wash and dry dishes," he added teasingly.

Sara gave a shrug then she burst out laughing. "You're going to regret telling me that," she told him. She stopped, caught by the expression on his face. "What?"

"I had forgotten how much your laughter lights up your face," he murmured. "You're incredibly beautiful, do you know that?"

"Thanks David," she reached for his hand on the table and squeezed it gently. "Thanks for another chance."

"You're welcome," he said huskily.

Sara ordered the deep fried lobster and tossed vegetables and David had the lobster in lemon juice and sweet potatoes. They talked and he told her that this was one of the restaurants he supplied to; so he gets a special discount.

They finished off with wine and chocolate mousse that had her mouth watering. They left shortly after and Sara found her heart hammering again; which was ridiculous because this was David, fancy clothes aside, this was her David that she had known and who had taken her virginity all those years ago; the same David she had made love with several nights ago.

He took her wrap as soon as they were inside. "Want something to drink?" he asked her, his hands still lingering on her shoulders.

Sara shook her head no and turned around to face him. "I want you," she told him bluntly. She had stepped out of her rose colored heels and had to look up at him.

David stared at her; he had gone still. Then he pulled her against him. "I kept telling myself it was no use dreaming of her, she is way out of you league, she was too beautiful; she deserves some rich executive, who could give her anything she wanted. I spent the years after you had gone, killing myself to become that rich executive and would one day claim you and prove that I was man enough to keep you. Ironically, I managed to amass a comfortable living but I did not want to be an executive; I hate the suits and offices make me claustrophobic. I love you and I hope it's enough for you." He bent his head, his breath stirring against her lips, and then he took hers slowly, deliberately, his tongue touching hers, playing with hers. But Sara wanted more. She wrapped her arms around his neck and brought her body closer to his; capturing his tongue with hers. He groaned inside her mouth, his arms tightening around her small waist. He reached for the zipper at the back of her dress and slid it down; Sara pulled away from him and stepped out of the dress.

"I was wondering all night what you had on underneath that dress," he said ruefully, his hand reaching out to touch her small round breasts. Her panties were so minute that it showed much more than it hid. He lifted her and carried her up to the bedroom, placing her on the bed. He quickly took off his clothes and Sara found herself staring at his aroused penis;

and as he climbed back on the bed she reached for it; running her hand up and down its length.

"Sara," he murmured huskily, hovering over her. He bent his head and put his mouth on one of her breasts; circling the nipple with his tongue. Sara gasped and arched her back; she had let go of his erection and had dug her hands in his dark hair. He moved to give the other one his full attention. By this time, Sara was moving restlessly under him; the pressure building up inside her.

"David please," she gasped, almost pulling his hair from the root. He released her breast and came over her, going down the length of her stomach to her pubic area. "No," she muttered, uttering a sharp cry as his tongue touched her before plunging inside, working deep inside her, savoring her essence. Sara was almost hysterical with need and she begged him to take her.

He knelt over her and guided his erection inside her wet warmth. She closed around him like a vice and with a deep moan he started moving inside her. Sara wrapped her legs around his waist, her hands reaching up to clasp his neck. "I love you," she cried out.

He went still and Sara looked at him in confusion. "Say it again," he demanded hoarsely.

"I love you," she repeated hoarsely.

"You've never said that to me before," he told her softly. "Tell me again, please"

"I love you David Graham," she kissed him softly on his lips. His penis was pulsing inside her and she felt as if she could stay that way forever. "I love you."

With a shudder, he took her lips roughly, his hips moving rapidly against hers. She matched his thrusts with hers, her body on fire for him. She wanted more, so much more of him; she could not get enough. He gave her all of him, not holding back; he held her to him; not wanting to let go as he showed her with his body what he was afraid to say with his voice. They came together, their cries mingling together inside the room. David shuddered with the magnitude of his pleasure and even when he had emptied himself inside her, he could not stop, could not let her go.

Sara combed her fingers through his soft dark hair as he rested his forehead on hers; trying to control his breathing. "I can't move," he told her softly.

"I don't want you to," she murmured.

"Good, I don't want to either," he sighed.

"When are you going to make a decent woman out of me?" she asked him casually as he rained soft kisses on her cheek. She felt the stiffening of his body and she knew she had caught him off guard. He had told her he loved her but she knew as far as asking her to marry him; she would have to bring that up.

"What are you saying?" he whispered, his head rearing up to look at her.

"I am saying that I love you and I want to be your wife David." She held his face with both her hands. "I am saying that I want us to live together as husband and wife."

He took a deep shuddering breath. "Are you sure?" he asked her, his eyes intense. "When we do this, there is no turning back Sara, no saying to me that you want to go and explore; I won't let you go again without me, so are you sure?"

"I am absolutely sure," she told him with a smile; one hand caressing his strong jaw and the growth of dark hair there. "It took me leaving you to know that there is not and never will be another man for me but you and I want to stay here with you and be your wife."

"I have waited so long to hear you say that," he muttered. "I love you so much Sara that I don't know how to behave around you sometimes. I am vulnerable around you and I want you to be my wife baby."

She captured his mouth with hers; her tongue touching his and inviting his touch. David sighed with pleasure and deepened the kiss; his mouth moving over hers slowly. He felt himself hardening inside her and he started moving slowly, one hand reaching down to cup her hip; guiding her against him as she moved, taking as well as giving.

He continued kissing her even when he had emptied himself inside her; waiting for her to reach her peak and when she did, he captured her cries inside his mouth; his body moving against hers in unison. They fell asleep shortly after and woke up at about a quarter to eleven, still in each other's arms.

"How about two weeks from now?" he asked her lazily, they had reversed positions and she was lying on top of him while he gently ran a hand down her back.

"Are you kidding me, David Graham?" she asked him, lifting her head to look at him.

"Too long?" he teased her, lifting his head to nip her chin with his teeth.

"Try again," she told him darkly.

"Three weeks," he murmured. "Three weeks, Sara," he reiterated as she made about to protest. "I am not waiting any longer."

Sara looked at the determined expression on his face and smiled in acceptance. "Three weeks it is, I'll try and work my miracle."

"Nothing big," he told her.

"Good luck with that," she informed him. "Our church family will all expect to be at our wedding darling and who are we to say no?"

"Say it again," he murmured huskily.

"What?" she stared at him puzzled.

"Darling," he clarified.

"My darling, my love," she murmured, staring into his eyes.

With a broken sigh he brought her head down to his and claimed her lips in a devastatingly tender kiss.

*****

He took her home the next morning and came in with her. She was going to get ready for church while he spoke with her father; he was already dressed for church.

"Hi Dad," she kissed her father on the cheek as he came in the living room to greet them. He was still in his bathrobe and had on his socks and slippers which meant he was in the process of getting ready for church.

She hurried upstairs to put on her church clothes, she had already showered at David's. She smiled as she remembered how long the shower had taken because in between they had made love several times.

With a frown of concentration she opened her closet door; looking for something suitable. David had told her that he was going to ask pastor to announce their upcoming nuptials at church today and he had called his parents and given them the good news. Sara had made sure and called Callie and told her that she expected her to be her maid of honor. Her friend had squealed loud in her excitement and had told her it was about time.

She decided on a pale green figure hugging dress with a slim hem. It had small cap sleeves and the fabric was soft and clingy. She added white accessories and white heels with a minimum amount of make-up.

There was a knock on the door and she turned to see her father framed in the doorway. He was already dressed and had his Bible in his hand. "I am ready now dad," she told him, picking up her white clutch from the dressing table.

"I have just been told the good news," he told her, his eyes glistening with tears. "I am a very proud father, my dear and could not ask for a better son. That young man is going to make you a fine husband."

"Thanks Dad, I know," she reached up and fixed his tie. "I just want you to know I have no intention of leaving again and I won't leave you alone."

"I know that my dear," he told her with a smile. "Now let's go down before your young man gets impatient." He took her arm and they walked downstairs together.

David stared at the picture she made as she approached him. "I never can get over how incredibly beautiful you are," he whispered as he took her hand in his. He was driving his car and her father was going to go in his.

"You had better not," Sara whispered back, as she tightened her hand in his. She could not believe how happy she was and could not help comparing today to that Sunday several months ago when she had just came back and was going to church; how lost she had been. Now she was about to get married to the man of her dreams and she had to thank God for that.

www.SaucyRomanceBooks.com/RomanceBooks

*****

There was a flurry of excitement when their wedding was announced at church. David had insisted she sit beside him up front and Pastor Phillips had bid them to come up to the altar while he prayed God's blessing on their union.

There were so many well wishers coming over to congratulate them and asked what the arrangement was. David's mother had pulled her aside and gave her a quick hug. "You have made my son very happy my dear," she smiled. "And I expect a few grandchildren later on," she grinned.

Sara blushed and hugged her. "Thanks for your forgiveness."

"Nothing to it," Sally linked her hand through hers. "Now about the catering…"

Callie came over as soon as she had finished discussing the catering with Sally who offered to stand the cost and deal with the whole aspect of it and had waved away Sara's protests. "My only child is getting married, it's the least I can do," she had told her.

"You expect to plan a wedding in three weeks?" Callie demanded, dragging her away from David, who had pulled her in beside him as soon as she had finished talking to his mother. "What world are you living in?"

"It can be done," Sara told her firmly, "We will be looking for the dresses tomorrow and Sister McLean and Sis. Bryan has offered to decorate the church. The reception will be in the church hall. We do not want a big wedding Callie; we just want to start our lives together and we want to do it properly."

"Okay, fine," Callie said resignedly. "Pick me up in the morning. I will take Benjamin over to Paul's mother's for the day and I expect a huge lunch," the girl warned.

"You will get nothing less," Sara grinned at her.

"Congratulations girl, I am so happy for you." She hugged Sara tightly before going over to her husband.

"Hey you," David came up behind her and pull her back into his arms. "I have something for you."

"What is it?" she asked him curiously, turning around in his arms.

"You'll see," he told her mysteriously.

They left church shortly after and she told her father she would be home later on. He had waved her away and told her with a smile that he is supposed to give way to her husband to be.

David took her to his parents' home. His mother was still at church because she was organizing some garden party with several of the women. His father hugged her as soon as she came through the door. He was still suffering from a bad back and could only hobble around but he promised that even if he had to be put in a wheelchair, he was going to be at the wedding.

David took her up to his old room. "Couldn't we have made out at your house?" she teased him as she sat on the bed while he pulled open a desk drawer.

"You're insatiable," he told her dryly. He had a black velvet box in his hand and as he approached her, Sara's breath caught inside her throat. He went down on his knees in front of her. "I bought this the week before you left. It took all of my savings but I wanted the best for you and I kept it even when you left." He opened the box and Sara gasped, her hand going to her throat. The single diamond solitaire flashed and sparkled in its white gold settings; it was exquisite.

"Oh David," she murmured tearfully. "Why didn't you tell me?"

"I was too proud and when you said you were leaving, I did not fight for you. I am not going to let you go again Sara," he warned her softly.

"I am not leaving," she reached out a hand and touched his cheek lovingly.

"Sara Williams, will you do me the great honor of being my wife?" he asked her gently, taking the ring from the box.

"I would be honored to," she told him holding out her left hand for him to put the ring on her finger. It was a perfect fit and she sat there admiring the diamond on her slim finger. He stood up and pulled her up against him.

"You have just made me the happiest man in the world," he told her, reaching for her lips. Sara closed her arms around his neck and leaned into him; returning his kiss with a passion that shook them to the very core. He felt himself hardening against her and he wanted to take her then and there but had to fight for control as he remembered that his father was downstairs.

He broke off the kiss and rested his forehead against hers; his breathing rapid. "I love you so much," he murmured, hugging her to him.

They stayed that way until they were calm enough to go back downstairs. Sara found the tears shimmering in her eyes as she leaned her head against his shoulder. This was where she belonged.

Chapter 8

The dress shopping proved exhausting and not productive. The only bridal shop in the small town had dresses that were either outdated or totally unsuitable.

Callie and Sara had spent the entire afternoon searching through the racks without success. They decided to go and get some lunch and consider their next option. They went to the 'Fish Place' and ordered fish and chips which they ate with gusto. Her father had told Sara to take the week off and he would be able to manage without her.

"If we don't find anything at the next store I can always find something buried in my closet that's suitable for the occasion." Callie said. The little restaurant was crowded and she waved at a few people she recognized.

Sara gripped her hands; her eyes lighting up with excitement. "I am an idiot!" she exclaimed, pushing away her half eaten plate of food.

"I would agree if I knew why it is," Callie said with a puzzled look at the other girl.

"Apart from the money I made modeling, there was an added bonus. I got to keep all the clothes I modeled and one of them was an incredibly beautiful white dress that I wondered at the time, where on earth was I going to wear this to. And there is also a sapphire blue dress that would look perfect on you."

"Then I do concur, you are an idiot," Callie said, the excitement catching on. "Let's go raid your closet."

They went home immediately and Sara went straight to her closet. Callie's eyes widened at the amount of clothes she saw; it was like she was looking at a rainbow. "What on earth are you doing with so many clothes?" she asked incredulously, running her over the different fabrics and styles.

"I happen to love clothes and shoes," Sara said defensively. "I have no problem sharing." She added with a smile.

"Good," Callie grinned, pulling out a dress in wild red and one in dark blue. "I love these."

"They're yours," Sara said generously. She pulled out the white dress she had told Callie about and held it up for her inspection. The other girl gasped in wonder, her eyes wide as she stared at the beautiful creation. It was off white and knee length with narrow hem. It was elegant in its simplicity and the bodice had pearls stitched in from the bosom to the waist and had small capped sleeves. It was deceptively simple until Sara tried it on and it took on a life of its own, molding and hugging her perfectly, giving her an ethereal beauty. Callie's gaze was transfixed and she could not tear her eyes away from her friend.

"David's going to die along with every man attending the wedding," Callie said dryly.

Sara laughed and walked over to her shoes closet, taking out off white heels with a bow at the side. "What do you think?"

"Perfect," Callie said in approval. "What about accessories?"

"I have tons of those," Sara hurried over to a huge jewelry box on her dressing table and took out a single strand of pearls; delicately made drop earrings and a slim bracelet.

"You're all set," Callie nodded in approval. "And we could put some tiny white rosebuds at one side of your hair.

"Now it's your turn," Sara went to the closet and searched until she found a sapphire blue dress with flared waist and fitted bodice. "It's kind of short on me but I am taller than you are, so it's perfect." Callie tried it on hurriedly, gazing in the mirror at the transformation. "What a fabulous dress can do to you," she sighed, running a hand lovingly over the soft satin fabric.

"I also have accessories to match." Sara told her, digging through her jewelry box. She handed Callie a sparkling faux sapphire necklace the stones shimmering with light and a matching set of earrings. They decided they would dress at Sara's since everything was already there. They sat among the clothes strewn on the bed and chatted idly about the plans for the wedding.

"Absolutely no shower," Sara said firmly, tucking her feet underneath her as she leaned back against the pillows. "David doesn't want a bachelor's party; I am just going to take that night to rest and spend some time with Dad. I am also going to be moving some stuff over to David during that week and of course you'll be spending the night."

"Yes ma'am," Callie grinned at her. She was lying on her side at the foot of the bed. "I am so glad you are back and we are best friends again, I've missed you."

"I missed you too," Sara told her sincerely. "I never knew you could feel so alone in a big city with so many people around but that's exactly what I was, alone and lonely. I thought I was tired of a small town where people knew each other but I was wrong. I love this place and the familiarity of it."

"I know what you mean," Callie said soberly. "I always knew I belonged here and this is where I wanted to stay so I never had the mixed feelings like you did. I am glad you found where you belong Sara and if you had not gone you would be wondering and pining after the unknown."

"Thanks Callie," she told the girl softly.

Callie left shortly after; saying that she had to pick up Benjamin from her mother-in-law's and that she would be helping with the decoration of the church and the auditorium.

David called her at around three. "Hey baby," he said warmly. "How was your day?"

"Very productive," Sara told him. "How was yours?"

"Hectic," he said wryly. "Because of all the attention I have been focusing on you, my businesses have been suffering. I am afraid I won't be able to keep you in the lap of luxury you have gotten used to."

"No problem, I'll tough it out if I have to," she said in a mock serious tone. "As long as I am with you."

"Good answer," he said huskily. "I wish I could see you later but I have some things to do and they can't wait."

"I understand darling," she soothed. "I'll see you tomorrow."

"I love it when you call me darling," he told her huskily.

"Then I'll continue to do so, darling," she murmured.

"I'll call you later baby, I love you."

"I love you too." She murmured before hanging up.

*****

She was humming in tune to a popular song on the radio and grilling chicken for dinner when her phone rang.

She did not recognize the number but murmured a tentative hello. She had often wondered if Michael would ever try and get in touch with her and every time the phone rang since she had gotten back and it showed a strange number she had answered tentatively.

"Hello baby girl," She stiffened. She did not recognize the voice but the only person she remembered calling her baby girl was her mother.

"Who is this?" she asked sharply, her heart beating loudly.

"It's your mama, baby girl." The person continued.

Sara's first instinct was to hang up and she gripped phone tightly against her ear; her eyes closed. She had never expected to hear from her mother again and she did not know what to say to her.

"I know you probably don't want to talk to me but I want you to listen, baby girl," her voice was persuasive and Sara remembered her as an incredibly beautiful woman who turned heads wherever she went.

"I am listening," she told her coldly.

There was silence at the other end and Sara was almost wishing that she had ended the call. "I did not want to disturb your life but I felt I had to clear the air before your big day." She paused and Sara frowned wondering how she had heard about her impending nuptials. "I called your father," she said softly as if reading Sara's thoughts. "I don't want you to end up like me Sara; I left the love of a wonderful man because I thought I was too good for him and the town we lived in and I wanted better. There was no better and I found that out the hard way. I knew you went away for a time and you came back and David still loved you, so you're fortunate and I want you to know that."

Sara was silent for a spell. Her mother's story sounded so much like hers only she had been granted a second chance. She felt her heart constricting in pity. "Why didn't you come back?"

"Because it was too late for me," the voice sounded incredibly weary and sad. "I went and lived with a man who showed me a very glamorous lifestyle and he kept telling me we would get married eventually, until I got pregnant and had a miscarriage and found out he had no further use for me. I have made my mistakes and I am living with the result of it; there is no turning back for me. I only called to wish you all the best and I know you'll be very happy."

"Thanks er – Mom," she said uncertainly. She had spent so much time hating and being angry with her mother that she had no idea how to feel now. "Do you want to come to the wedding?"

"No, baby girl," she said ruefully. "I don't belong there anymore and I don't want to spoil your big day. All I'm asking is that I get to keep in touch with you."

"I think I would like that," she told her softly.
"Thanks baby girl," Caroline whispered and hung up the phone.

*****

Her father came home and found her in the same place in the darkened kitchen. She had finished preparing the meal but her appetite was non-existent and she was deep in thought. She no longer felt the burning resentment she had felt for her mother; her story was too sad. She had messed up so bad that she could not find her way back

She blinked as her father switched on the light. "Girl what are you doing in the dark?" he asked her, placing his leather bag on the chair nearest the door.

"Hi dad, are you hungry?" she asked automatically.

"Starving," he told her, taking a seat. "What's the matter?"

"Mom called," she said casually, getting up and busying herself by making a plate.

"Yes?" he paused in the middle of putting a piece of meat into his mouth.

"You don't sound the least bit surprised," she carried her plate to the table and sat next to him.

"She called me earlier and I told her you were getting married and she cried." Her father put down his fork and linked his hands together. "What did you say to her?"

"You mean, did I tell her to get off my phone and never call me again?" she asked, with raised brows.

"Something like that," he told her ruefully.

"You really love her don't you?" Sara looked at her father astutely.

"I told you love is not something you switch on and off." Her father said gently.

"Why didn't you fight for her Dad?" Sara asked earnestly. "Why did you give up on her?"

"I begged her to come back, even when I found out she was pregnant with the man's child and even after she miscarried and she called me crying, I begged her to come back but she told me that she was too far gone to come back. I tried fighting but I just gave up and left it alone. I am here if and when she needs me." He told her.

"Oh Dad," Sara cried, reaching out a hand to touch his. "Why didn't you tell me?"

"Because it's between me and your mother, dear and I strongly feel that God will sort it out in his own time and his own way." He told her gently.

"You are an amazing man, do you know that?" she asked him, tears in her eyes. "I hope I can be half the person you are."

"You already are," he told her softly, leaning forward to kiss her cheek.

www.SaucyRomanceBooks.com/RomanceBooks

*****

That night when David called her she told him everything. "You okay baby?" he asked anxiously. "Want me to come over?"

"I am okay darling," she told him gratefully. "I just did not know a lot of things and now I know. I feel so sorry for her David and I shudder to think that what happened to her almost happened to me. I almost lost you."

"But you didn't," he told her firmly. "I love you baby and soon we are going be together for the rest of our lives."

"I know David and I love you so much. I am going to spend the rest of my life showing you." She told him tearfully.

"I am going to hold you to that," he told her teasingly. "Get some sleep baby, I'll see you tomorrow."

She did not sleep right away. She could not get her mother out of her mind. How sad she must be. She had left a wonderful, loving man and had run away to something that was shallow and meaningless. She sounded so miserable and sad and Sara felt all of her resentment floating away. Her father still loved her so much and he was not bitter and he still listened to her and talked with her and had told her about her daughter's upcoming wedding. What a love. A love that transcends all wrongs and distance; she realized with a sharpness that hit her that it was the kind of love David had for her. He had loved her even when she had deserted him and even though he had fought it; it had still been there.

With a sudden decision; she picked up her phone and dialed his number. "Baby, you okay?" he answered immediately.

"Thank you," she told him softly, well aware that she had probably woke him up.

"For what?" his voice was puzzled.

"For loving me even when I didn't deserve it," she said huskily.

"You always deserved it," he told her softly. "Don't ever think that. We all make mistakes and I would never hold that against you. I will always love you no matter what."

"I don't know what I did to deserve you but I am going to run with it." She smiled through her tears. "I love you David Graham, now go back to sleep."

"As if I could now," he told her dryly. "Goodnight baby." He said before he hung up.

*****

Deacon Williams opened his Bible and took out the picture, dog eared due to numerous handlings. It was a picture of him and Caroline that they had taken more than twenty years ago. It was a picture full of promises, sunshine and love. She was looking up at him; her head thrown back as she laughed at something he had said; he was looking down at her with a big grin on his face and all the love he felt for her showed on his face. Her striking resemblance to their daughter was highlighted. Caroline's beauty was such that you had to take several looks and you could not look away. His hand moved over her still form in the picture, taking in her coffee and cream complexion and her shoulder length dark brown curls. Her mother had been half white and Caroline had a mixture that made her beauty exotic and she had passed it on to her daughter. He had often pinched himself, wondering what such a beautiful woman saw in a plain Joe like him. He had worshiped her and had done everything her way because he had been so afraid of losing her. But that had been the wrong thing to do; she held immense power over him and she had wielded it mercilessly.

He had watched her get progressively unhappy each day and had chosen to ignore it, trying harder to fix what was wrong inside her but he had gradually realized that he could not fix her. When she had said she wanted to leave, he had let her, he told himself he had no right to stop her.

He replaced the picture and closed the Bible. He was no longer pining over her but he was still in love with her and that would never change. Now he was contented and was so happy that his daughter was marrying such a wonderful man; he had been so afraid that she was so like her mother and her leaving had reinforced that feeling. Now she was back and he praised God that she had gotten whatever it was out of her system.

He went to his desk drawer and took out the deed to the store. He had had his lawyer draw up papers; he was turning over the store to her. It was time to hang up his hat and let her run the show; he needed to slow things down and she had proven that she could more than manage. It was going to be his wedding gift to her. With a whimsical smile he placed the deed on the dresser and reached for the phone. He had failed to tell his daughter that Caroline had been calling him every night and they had been talking.

She answered on the first ring. "Hey, I thought you weren't going to call," her husky melodious voice still had the power to quicken his old heart.

"Not a chance," he settled back against the pillow, a smile on his face.

"I spoke to our daughter today," she told him tentatively.

"I know," he answered. "I am glad you finally did, I told you she would not reject you."

"I messed up so bad. I feel so ashamed and now I have to stay in the background while our daughter is having the biggest day of her life." She murmured sadly.

"So come home," he told her. He had been telling her that for some time now; but she had always found some excuses. "I am sure she would be happy to see you Caro,"

"I keep thinking about what those church folks will say when they see me," she laughed shakily. She had told him that she lived on her own now in some tiny apartment and was working at an old people's home.

"Why do you care so much about what people say?" he asked her impatiently. "They will talk for a little bit and then they will find other subjects to move on to. I think you owe your daughter something Caro. Maybe this can be a way of paying her back somewhat." He had been telling her the same thing every week and he hoped this time she would listen. He also had a selfish reason, God forgive him, he thought grimly but he wanted to see her; even just for a little bit.

"I'll think about it," she promised him and he felt his heart quickened. She had never said that before; so now there was hope.

"So how have you been?" he asked her in concern. The last time they spoke she had not been doing so well, she had been recovering from a particularly nasty bout of the flu.

"I am recovering slowly, thanks," she said gratefully. She had always wondered how he could still love her when she had messed up so bad; but she realized that she had left what was a rare love to go and search for something that was common;

something that fizzle out at the first sign of a conflict. She wished she could go back but pride and shame held her back.

"Have you been drinking a lot of liquid?" he asked her anxiously and Caroline smiled. It felt so good for a change to have someone looking out for her. Why did she feel she had to leave that? What kind of a fool was she that she had left something so wonderful to look for God knew what?

"Yes, doctor," she teased. Then she changed the subject and she told him about an old lady she was looking after at the home. The one who had not one relative coming to look for her and how she had been spending a lot of time with her.

They talked way into the night and Deacon felt the tenderness enveloping him as he listed to her. He loved her and that was never going to stop.

Chapter 9

Sara came down to the kitchen the next morning to find her father sitting at the breakfast table eating cereal and a glass of orange juice beside him. There was an official looking document on her side of the table. She had decided she was going in to work today no matter what her father said. Her wedding was this weekend and no matter what her father said she needed to get some things done.

"What's this?" she asked him, puzzled as she poured herself some orange juice.

"Why don't you open it and see?" Her father said mysteriously, putting down the paper he had been perusing.

She did and what she saw made her eyes widen in shock. "Dad?" She looked from the paper to him.

"It's your wedding present," he told her with a smile.

"Dad, are you sure?" Sara asked him huskily.

"Absolutely," he told her cheerfully, standing and coming over to give her a hug. "I need to relax and do nothing for a while. It's time for me to step down and let you run things. I will be there until after your wedding and if you're planning on going on any honeymoon."

"Is there something you're not telling me? Are you sick?" her tone was one of alarm. She looked up at him, her brow creased in concern.

"I am as fit as a fiddly dear girl," he gave her a quick squeeze before letting go. "Accept it for what it is, honey; a gift."

"Oh Dad," she breathed; going over and hugging him from behind. "I have so many things I want to do. A reading corner in the back, and a homework center –"

"Whoa there, slow down girl," her father laughed affectionately. "For now you need to concentrate on your upcoming wedding,"

"Thanks Dad, I love you so much." She told him, putting a gentle hand on his rough cheek.

"I didn't ask you if that was what you wanted to do," there was concern on his lined face.

"It's what I want to do Dad, don't worry, I am not going anywhere," she told him astutely.

"I know honey, I know." He kissed her cheek softly. "Okay let's get out of here, for now I am still your boss."

Sara laughed and quickly downed her juice and they left together.

*****

She showed David the deed that night. She had started moving some things over to the house that was going to be theirs and had decided to leave the heavy stuff for the night before the wedding. He had cooked her dinner and even though he had been busy digging up dirt to do some replanting and transplanting he had told her to relax while he cooked dinner. They had showered together and had spent so much time in the bathroom that their skin had turned wrinkled by the time they had got out. It was four days to the wedding and Sara could not wait.

They were sitting outside on the porch swing eating chocolate chip ice-cream; the sun was still high in the sky even though it was almost seven o'clock. David had pulled her back against him, intermittently feeding her from his bowl.

"So how do you feel about being the owner of a thriving business?" he asked her softly.

She leaned back her head to stare at him. He was so earthy and good-looking that she got weak just looking at him "I feel like a business woman," she told him loftily with a smile.

He bent his head and kissed her mouth; cold by the ice-cream. "So I suppose I won't be expecting suppers in the evenings because my wife will be busy running a business?" he growled mockingly.

"You better believe it," she told him a mock serious expression on her face.

"In four days you will be my wife and I just can't wrap my head around it," he took the empty bowl from her and placed it along with his on the table next to the porch. "I keep asking myself if this is really happening and sometimes I wake up in a panic thinking that you are gone again."

Sara twisted around in his arms, her eyes troubled. "David do you believe I love you absolutely?" she asked him anxiously. "I am here with you because I want to be and nothing else. I love you so much that I can't breathe when you're near and I cannot sleep when you are not with me. I am not going anywhere please get that through your head."

"Sara," he touched her face gently. "I love you too and I am trying to get used to that." He laughed ruefully. "I have you right here in my arms and I cannot get over it. You're beautiful Sara, so much so that you take my breath away and ironically, because you don't realize how beautiful you are it makes you so much more appealing."

"Thank you, kind sir," she said impishly, gripping his face between her hands and kissing his lips. "Want to know what I think about you? I think you're the most handsome, most wonderful man I have ever met and aside from my father, you're on the top of my list, no one comes close and I am so honored to be with you and I can't wait to be your wife."

He kissed her hungrily and Sara felt the tears on his cheeks. She reached up a hand and touched it tenderly; this strong beautiful man was not afraid to show weakness in front of her. He was her man and she loved him so much that it hurts.

He picked her up and carried her gently to the bedroom and showed her how much he really loved her.

www.SaucyRomanceBooks.com/RomanceBooks

*****

They had the rehearsal dinner at David's parents' home. Sally had offered to do the dinner because she wanted to play her part in their wedding. It was Thursday night at eight p.m. and apart from her and her father, Pastor Phillips, Callie and her husband Paul was going to be there as well as David's best man; Bradford Miller.

She was spending the night at David's house after so she had dressed from there and they had left together. He had told her it was her home too and she was to feel free to redecorate; except his study; he liked it just the way it was.

The dinner was going well. Sally had outdone herself in the catering; offering several dishes and a large strawberry and vanilla cake with their names on it. "I didn't get to throw you an engagement party so consider this as being one." She told them with a smile.

"I want to make a toast," she continued, standing and lifting her glass that was halfway full of the red wine she had provided. "David and Sara's love affair spanned a number of years. Their love has overcome so many obstacles and has only grown stronger and I am so happy for them. I am not losing my son, I am gaining a beautiful daughter and I want to offer my sincerest blessings and to let them know that our prayers," she glanced at her husband, "Will always be with them. To the happy couple; cheers." She lifted her glass in toast and the others followed suit.

There were choruses of cheers all around. A number of toasts followed including her father who said that he always knew they were going to end up together; a love like that could never be over. Sara stared at him for a moment as he sat back down, her expression thoughtful.

Sally took her arms as they were mingling in the living room and took her into the kitchen. "I need help with the dessert, I know it's your night but I want to say something to you."

Sara felt a little apprehensive. The relationship between her and Sally was still a little tenuous.

"Oh my dear," Sally laughed as she took out the cake knife. "Don't look like that, I have no hang ups where you're concerned. I actually like you and David would have my head if I say one bad thing against you. No," she pointed to the cake plates on the counter, "I just want to say I am sorry for attacking you in the store that day. I was wrong and it was me playing interfering mama. I am glad you are in David's life and I can see he would never be happy with anyone else but you."

"Thanks Sally," Sara said grateful. "I hurt him so much before because I was so foolish and I won't ever do that again. I love him so much."

"I know dear," Sally said softly; placing the slices of cake on the plates.

"Is this a private party or can anyone join in?" David's voice was casual but his eyes searching as he came up behind Sara and pulled her back into his arms.

"Darling, Sara and I were just talking mother to daughter," Sally told him with a quick smile.

"Yes we were," Sara angled her head to look up at him and was rewarded with a quick kiss.

"Nothing to worry about, Sara and I are going to get along like a house on fire," Sally came over and hugged them both. "Very soon we will be talking grandchildren." With a merry laugh she went back into the living room; leaving David staring down at Sara with amusement.

"Any thoughts?" he asked her teasingly.

"None whatsoever," she told him firmly.

That night when they went home and were lying in each other's arms after they had made love, Sara brought it up. "I wish she would come back to him," she said musingly; trailing a hand over his chest, fiddling with his chest hair. They were both naked; neither of them bothering to put on clothes.

"Who are we talking about?" David asked lazily, running his hand down her back.

"My Mom and Dad," Sara told him, shivering as his touch sent off shivers down her spine.

"Ah," David said with a smile. "What brought that on?"

"I have been doing a lot of thinking David and the comment he made tonight about love like that never ending, I think he was referring to their love or rather his love for her." She raised her head to look down at him.

"So you want to play matchmaker?" he queried with a raised brow.

She shrugged one slim shoulder. "Everybody deserves a second chance, he said that to me and so did you."

"You're right," he nodded. "But sometimes you have to let people deal with that sort of thing for themselves baby; even if they are your parents."

"I guess you're right," Sara sighed, resting her head back on his chest. "It's just that I hate that he's going to be alone when I am living here with you, I kind of wished he had someone there with him."

"You father will manage and who knows what the future holds?" David reassured her. "You say they talk all the time, don't you?" Sara nodded. "Things have a way of coming full circle. You came back to me didn't you?" he asked her softly.

She shook her head yes. "Would you have taken me back if I was pregnant with another man's child?" she asked him quietly.

"I would have loved you if you had ten children," he told her wryly. "I love you unconditionally Sara and you have to realize that it's not based on what you did or did not do. I love you and that's it. Full stop. Period."

"Dad said the same thing about Mom," she murmured. "Oh David!" she cried, sliding on top of him. "I am so blessed."

*****

"This is the last load," Brad came in, his arms filled with flowers of all different colors; white roses, gardenias and bluebells predominant. David was busy filling orders for several customers so Brad had offered his services as delivery person. "Anything else?"

"Not right now Brad," Sally told him, her eyes sweeping the huge auditorium. The blue and white balloons were already up all over the room and Callie was busy decorating the podium where the head table was going to be. They had told Sara to go home and soak in a long hot bath as tomorrow was going to a big day for her but she had refused. She had told them if she went home she was just going to go stir crazy and some stupid tradition dictates that she could not see David.

"You cannot fight tradition girl," Callie warned her. They had been there since nine in the morning and had sent out to get pizza at one and they were still at it. Several church sisters were there as well and the work was going very well. Sara was barely allowed to do anything; which was very frustrating.

With a resigned sigh she decided to go to the store and spend some time with her dad; she was still so concerned about him being at home by himself.

"Okay, you win," She called out to them as she took up her huge pocket book and slung it over her shoulder. "I am leaving."

"No going to see David," Callie called out as she headed for the doorway. Sara made a face at her and went to her car.

*****

"My dear what on earth are you doing here?" her father looked up as the doorbell tinkled. There were a few people milling around and he was standing by the non-fiction section looking at some titles.

"Not even my own father wants me around?" Sara asked in exasperation, going to the office to put down her pocket book.

"I always want to see you," he told her as soon as she came back out. "But today you're supposed to be resting and pampering yourself for tomorrow." He returned her hug.

"Sally, Callie and the others won't allow me to lift a finger," she complained and David is busy getting off orders before tomorrow."

"You're not supposed to," he smiled and waved at a woman as she left the store and came and sat beside Sara.

"I guess I am just feeling a little useless," she told him ruefully.

"Tomorrow will be here before you know it," he reassured her. "I know," she smiled. "Dad what was it like when you and Mom got married?"

Her father looked at her for a moment and then holding up a hand, he went to serve a customer. He came back a few minutes later and by then the store was empty. He was planning to close earlier than usual to go home and get some rest before tomorrow and he had told his customers that he would be closed tomorrow.

He sat down beside her and folded his hands together, his expression far away. "She had me running around in circles," he said with a slight smile. "I met her when I was working at the fast food restaurant in town. She came in with a couple of friends and she stood out from among them; even though they were strikingly beautiful girls; Caroline stood out from among them. She radiated beauty and confidence but was very down to earth and approachable." He paused as if going back in time. "You're so much like her that it's uncanny," he added, turning to look at her. "I was nervous and never got up the courage to talk to her until the fourth time she came in and that time she was alone."

"Did she shut you down?" Sara asked fascinated.

Deacon Williams laughed softly. "What a way to put it," he said. "But no she did not and we talked and I asked her out. She did not quite say yes and she did not quite say no; she just said maybe and I kept asking and she kept coming, until she finally said yes and I took her to the movies. The first time I tried to kiss her, she slapped my face and refused to see me for a week." He laughed and Sara laughed with him.

"We went out for a year before I asked her to marry me, I didn't feel I was worthy enough to be her husband and I was shocked when she said yes and I was over the moon. I almost killed myself trying to acquire enough money to keep her in style and to give her a wedding I thought she deserved. I always thought she was marrying beneath her and I wanted to make up for that."

"Dad," Sara whispered reaching for his hands. "How could you think that?"

"I was an idiot in love and I believed it so much that I had her believing it too." He told her sadly. "And from the beginning the relationship was unbalanced. I kept trying too hard and I guess I smothered her; I just felt I had to prove myself worthy of her."

"Oh Dad, you are one of the most beautiful and generous men I know and I am sure Mom thinks that as well; you don't have to prove anything to anyone."

"I know that now honey," he told her sadly. "I know that we are all God's creatures and he made us all beautiful; some more than most," he added with a grin. "But I am okay with that." He stood up and gave her a gentle kiss on her cheek as she stood up with him. "I am going to be fine Sara, don't worry about me."

*****

That night at home; it was just the three of them; she, her father and Callie who kept calling her husband every five second to check up on their son. "It must be hard leaving your son with a stranger," Sara told her in amusement as she hung up from calling Paul for the fifth time since she had gotten to the house. They were in the living room and her father had gone to get a fresh bottle of non alcoholic wine.

"You just wait until you start having children," Callie warned her as she plopped down on the sofa beside Sara. "I can't believe that tomorrow at this time, you'll be Mrs. David Graham."

"I am still pinching myself," Sara agreed; nibbling on a tuna sandwich. David had called her a little while ago to say that he loved her and he could not wait until tomorrow.

"All right girls, here we go," Deacon Williams came back with the chilled bottle of wine and poured some in the glasses already there. "Here's to my lovely daughter who has found love that is so rare in this world today."

"Cheers," Sara and Callie said in unison. They drank in silence for a little while until her father decided it was time for him to turn in. "I'll leave you young people alone while I go get some sleep. Big day tomorrow," he said with a wink as he came and gave Sara a kiss on the cheek. "Don't stay up too late."

As soon as he was out of earshot Callie said, "I hope he's not going to be too lonely here by himself,"

"I said the same thing to him but he told me he was going to be fine." Sara had told Callie about her mother calling the other day. "I asked him about the time he first met mom and he told me. He really loves her Callie and he still does."

"Jeez!" she exclaimed; padding over to pour another glass of wine and to top up Sara's. "How sad it must be to love somebody so much and be apart from them." She added sympathetically.

"I think they will get back together one day," Sara said with confidence. Deep in her heart she hoped they would because in spite of what her father told her; he was going to be lonely.

"I hope so," Callie said contemplatively. "A love that spans time and distance; it sure makes for a good movie or a book," she grinned. "Here's to real true love," she lifted her glass and Sara lifted hers and they clinked their glasses together.

They retired to their bedrooms shortly after. Callie was staying in the guest bedroom and Sara brought her towels from the linen closet.

www.SaucyRomanceBooks.com/RomanceBooks

"Please let me do my job as matron of honor," Callie warned. "I am supposed to bring you breakfast in bed, so in order for you to get it in bed, you have to stay in bed."

"Yes mother," Sara grinned as she retired to her own bedroom. It took a while for her to sleep and when she did, she dreamed of weddings and honeymoons.

Chapter 10

She woke up very early the next morning but remembering the warning from Callie, she stayed in bed. Today she was getting married to the man she loved. She felt the quickening of her heartbeat. A glance at the bedside clock told her it was barely six o'clock and she did not expect her father and Callie to be awake yet.

Her cell phone rang just then and without looking at the caller id she knew who it would be. "Hi darling," she answered.

"I see you're wide awake," he said huskily. "How did you sleep?"

"It would have been better if I had been beside you," she told him softly, pulling herself up to recline against the pillows.

"Any trace of second thoughts?" he asked lightly but Sara could hear the trace of anxiety in his voice.

"Are you kidding?" she exclaimed. "I wish we were standing at the altar right now,"

"I am glad to hear that," he told her huskily. "I can't wait either."

"See you later," she whispered softly before hanging up.

Callie bustled in at a quarter to seven with a tray and white 'goo' on her face. "Love your new look," Sara teased as she took the tray from her friend.

"I don't happen to have flawless skin like you," she sniffed. "Make sure you eat everything on the plate." She told her before heading for the door. "Your dad and I will be eating breakfast now and I will come back and collect the tray."

The plate was packed with all of her favorite breakfast foods. There were scrambled eggs, bacon and cheddar; waffles with maple syrup and strawberries and whipped cream. There was also a cup of strong black coffee and a tall glass of orange juice.

To her surprise, Sara dug into the meal with gusto and ate everything; including the glass of orange juice and the coffee which she left for last. She was sipping it when Callie came back in to collect the tray.

"Pastor Phillips said we are not supposed to be late and I am to make sure that you get ready on time." Callie told her, putting the tray on the side table. "The fashionably late bride does not work for him."

"It does not work for me either, or David," Sara grinned, climbing out of bed. She had not seen her Dad and wanted to make sure he was okay. "Where is Dad?"

"In his room. I gave him a hearty breakfast and yes, I have called Paul two times since I got up, so sue me," she told Sara with a bland look.

"I won't say a word," Sara told her with a backward look as she headed for the door.

Deacon Williams was in his study reading his Bible. "Dad I just came to say good morning," she told him, pulling up a chair beside him. He placed a book marker between the pages he had been reading and looked up at her with a smile.

"This house will not be the same without you," he told her gently.

"Dad, please remember that I will not be far away and I promise to come over as often as I can," Sara said earnestly.

"Look at me child," he told her taking her hand inside his big warm ones. "I don't want you to go into your marriage, thinking you're responsible for me. I am going to be just fine; I have the good Lord with me always and I am not in the least bit lonely."

"I am just a phone call away, remember;" Sara told him tearfully, gripping his hands with hers.

"None of that on your wedding day," he told her firmly, gently wiping her cheeks. "I will be all right, you don't have to worry. Now run along and get ready, I don't want to have to answer to that young man of yours for making you late."

*****

By eleven thirty Callie was ready and helping her to get dressed. Sara had become an expert on putting on her own make-up and had insisted on doing so now. Callie had used hot curls in her short hair and there was a mass of curls around her beautiful face; there was also a sprig of white gardenias at the left side; placed strategically to fall down one delicate ear.

Next came the dress and Callie helped her slip over her sheer white teddy that molded her body lovingly.

She was sitting at the dressing table, retouching her make-up when she heard the voice at the doorway. "I never thought it possible but you are way more beautiful than I was at my wedding,"

Sara spun around, her lip gloss still in her hand. It was her mother. The woman whom she had not seen in fifteen years. Apart from looking a little thin and the wisps of gray in her own jet black hair she still looked beautiful. She had on a pearl gray skirt suit and matching shoes and a tiny hat that sat jauntily over her forehead. Her skin was flawless.

"Mom?" Sara stood up a little unsteadily.

"I will go and see what your father is up to," Callie said to no one in particular; hurrying towards the doorway, where she stopped to smile at the woman framed there. "Nice to see you again, Mrs. Williams."

"Thanks dear," Caroline returned the smile.

"I decided that it was time to come and see my daughter and what better time than on her big day?" she came further inside the room.

"Does dad know you're here?" Sara asked foolishly.
"He knew I was coming. I told him not to tell you, I wanted it to be a surprise," She reached out a hand to grasp her daughter's. "I hope it's a pleasant one,"

"I can't believe you're here," Sara said wonderingly.

"I am here and I don't want to make you late for your wedding. I just wanted to see you before you went to the church to find out your reaction about me being here." Caroline touched her cheek gently. "I didn't leave you baby girl, I pined every day for you but I thought I wanted more and I thought I was not ready to be a wife and a mother but I was so wrong. I am not asking you to forgive me now but I am asking for a second chance to be a mother to you."

"I have already forgiven you," Sara told her softly. "I just don't know how I feel about you but I guess it will take time. How long are you staying?"

"I am not sure – I"

"I have asked her to come home," her father's voice sounded just inside the doorway and both women turned to look at him. They were a twin set of beauties and his heart turned over inside him as he looked at them; they were visions to behold. "She has not answered me yet."

"Will you?" Sara asked her, turning back to stare at the woman who was an older version of her.

"I don't know yet, but I am not leaving tonight or maybe tomorrow night so we will see," Caroline said with a gentle smile, sending her ex-husband a warning look. "In the meantime, let's go get you married."

*****

Her mother rode with her and Callie in the rented limousine and all the way to the church, she held Sara's hand; every now and then fixing something in her hair or on her dress and staring at her as if she could not believe that she was actually seeing her. Sara had called David and told him about the addition to the guest list and he had said he was so happy for her.

Her mother and father walked her up the aisle and Sara felt rather than saw the curious looks they were getting and the whispers behind cupped hands but she had eyes only for her groom. He looked dashing in a dark blue suit with his dark hair combed back from his face.

He met her halfway up the aisle, shaking her father's hand and hugging her mother; welcoming her. Then he took Sara's hand; his eyes saying it all.

She handed Callie the flowers as soon as she reached where the rest of the party was and Pastor Phillips started the ceremony.

"Friends, we are gathered here today to be a witness to the joining together of our dear brother David and our sister Sara as they declare their love for each other before God and mankind. If there is anyone who thinks that this marriage should not take place; say it now or forever hold their peace." He waited a spell then continued in prayer.

"The parties have expressed their desire to say their own vows. So we will allow them to do so at this point." He indicated that David should start.

David took her hands in his. "Sara, you are my better half; you complete me and I do not want to live my life without you. I love God and then it's you; it has always been you and will always be you and no matter what happens from here on I will always love you."

"David, my love, my heart, you make me a better person; you make me want to be better and with you I have discovered a love that is so complete that I embrace it with all my being. It will always be you and no one else."

"I need not say anymore," Pastor Phillips said with a smile. "The rings please. David Graham do you take Sara Williams to be your lawful wife, forsaking all others until death do you part?"

"I do," David said soundly, sliding the ring onto Sara's finger.

"Sara, do you take David Graham to be your lawful husband to honor and obey until death do you part?"

"I do," Sara slid the ring onto his finger.

"Now by the power vested in me, I now pronounce you husband and wife. You may kiss your bride David."

He took her into his arms and kissed her gently, whispering to her, "My wife."

"Ladies and gentlemen, I now present to you Mr. and Mrs. David Graham" Pastor Phillips said as he bade the congregation to stand while the couple made their way down the aisle amide tremendous applause.

Sara met her mother's eyes and her own eyes teared up as she noticed the woman smiling at her and standing beside her father. The auditorium was in the same building but the wedding party was on their way to the park to take pictures.

They came back to the reception an hour later to find it in full swing. They were escorted to the head table and Sara found herself admiring the decorations on the table and the ceiling and walls. The cake was towering on a side table next to the head table. Sara searched for her mother and found her sitting with her father at the table several feet away from them. She was laughing at something Sara's father said and she was touching his arm. David's parents were sitting with them.

"They look happy don't they?" Sara asked David as she turned to see him looking at her.

"Yes, but I would like to have my wife's total attention." He told her in amusement.

"You said 'my wife' as if it's the most natural thing in the world," she murmured, angling her head to look at him, her husband.

"It is," he took her hand and brought it to his lips. "You're my wife."

Before she could respond the Master of Ceremonies stood and started talking. The toasts were made while they ate dinner and Sara found that she could barely eat. "You're going to need your strength for later," he whispered in her ear as she toyed with her food.

"I can hold my own," she retorted, poking her tongue out at him. To her shocked surprise he bent his head and took her tongue into his mouth. Sara barely heard the round of applause as she gave in to his melting kiss, her hand coming up to grasp his neck.

"Later," he whispered shakily as he released her lips.

They had the cutting of the cake and then it was time for their first dance as husband and wife.

"Have I told you that you're the most beautiful woman in this room?" he asked her as they danced to the tune of Luther Vandross' 'Here and now'.

"No, but you can tell me now," she looked up at him; her eyes sparkling with love for him. "My husband."

"My wife," he murmured, bending his head to take her lips with his. Sara forgot where they were, she forgot that there were other people around and she melted in his arms. She didn't want him to stop. The song had ended and they were still wrapped in each other's arms.

It was the clearing of somebody's throat that brought them back to the present. Her father was standing beside them; an indulgent expression on his face. "Mind if I borrow your wife?" he asked.

David grinned sheepishly, "Yes sir," he let go of her reluctantly and made his way over to his mother.

"We all thought you were getting a head start on your honeymoon," he said teasingly as he swung her around in time to the music.

"Dad!" Sara said with a blush.

"You are so beautiful and I am a proud father," he told her.

"Thanks dad," her gaze wandered over to where her mother was having a conversation with a sister from church. "Is she staying?" He did not have to ask who she meant.

"I still have hopes that she will," her father told her with a gentle smile.

"You're one amazing man, do you know that" Sara looked at her father with a gentle look.

"I have an amazing daughter," he murmured, giving her a kiss as the song ended. Sara watched as he made straight for her mother and the way her face lit up when she saw him. Suddenly, she knew that it was going to be all right; her father would not be alone.

She and David left shortly after; and her mother came over and hugged her, telling her that she would see her when they came back from their honeymoon. They were taking a road trip which would last a week. "So you're staying?"

"Your father gave a convincing argument," she sent a fond glance over to where he was talking to David's father. "I never really stopped loving him you know." She murmured.

"Oh Mom, that's great!" Sara hugged her tightly.

"Go on and start your marriage, your husband is waiting," she gave her daughter a soft kiss on the cheek.

David drove his car with the top down and they got home in record time. He lifted her and carried her straight upstairs to their bedroom. Some pieces of her furniture were now scattered around the room giving it a lived in look. He placed her gently on the floor. "We're home," he said softly. He took the sprig of flowers from her hair and Sara pulled out his bow tie.

"I love you David, my husband," she murmured, unbuttoning his shirt as he shrugged out of his jacket.

"I love you my wife Sara," he told her, his hands busy unzipping her dress; his eyes widening at the wisp of material she had on underneath. "It's a good thing I didn't know about this, I would have taken you then and there." He said ruefully, running a hand over the material covering her. He took off the rest of his clothes and when she made to take off her lingerie; he stopped her. "I want to do it," he said, standing before her gloriously naked, his erection throbbing. He lifted her and placed her gently on the bed and kneeling over her; he slowly peeled away the garment; revealing skin already flushed with desire.

Sara gasped as his mouth closed over one breast already hardened with the feelings rushing through her. His tongue licked and tasted and discovered. Then he moved over to the next one to give it the same treatment. His hand snaked between their bodies to dip inside her wet warmth; his fingers seeking and exploring. Sara was fast losing control of her emotions and as he delved deeper inside her, she felt the onslaught of emotions licking through her body like tongues of fire!

"David," she called out achingly, her hands grasping his soft dark hair. But he was not through with her yet as his mouth left her breast to continue on down to her stomach, lingering at her navel before making its way down to her pubic area. His tongue touched her there and caused her to jump and before she could recover he was inside her, licking and savoring and destroying her control. Her legs rose to give him further access and he gripped her hips, lifting and bring her closer to his mouth as he furiously brought her to a powerful orgasm that had her shaking uncontrollably!

He did not stop tasting her as he licked every drop from her, his tongue gentle yet persistent in its desire to give her extreme pleasure. It was then and only then; after he was satisfied that she was ready again for him that he climbed on top of her, positioning over her and guided his rigid penis inside her. She closed over him like a vise, taking him in; lifting her legs to wrap them around his waist as she prepared to give him her all.

"I love you so much," she told him shakily, her arms wrapping around his neck. "I don't ever want to be without you."

"You won't ever have to be," he told her huskily, his mouth, tasting of her, closing over hers as he started moving within her slowly at first then picking up the pace as she moved frantically underneath him, not satisfied with steady movements but wanting to give more, take more.

They came together as the tumultuous wave crashed over them; their cries mingling in the room as they expressed their love for each other; a love that had come full circle; a love that

www.SaucyRomanceBooks.com/RomanceBooks

was much more than physical but invaded their entire being as well.

The end.

If you enjoyed this book and want me to keep writing more, please leave a review of it on the store where you bought it. By doing so you'll allow me more time to write these books for you as they'll get more exposure. So thank you. :)

www.SaucyRomanceBooks.com/RomanceBooks

Get Free Romance eBooks!

Hi there. As a special thank you for buying this book, for a limited time I want to send you some great ebooks completely **free of charge** directly to your email! You can get it by going to this page:

www.saucyromancebooks.com/physical

You can see a the cover of these books on the next page:

www.SaucyRomanceBooks.com/RomanceBooks

www.SaucyRomanceBooks.com/RomanceBooks

These ebooks are so exclusive you can't even buy them. When you download them I'll also send you updates when new books like this are available.

Again, that link is:

www.saucyromancebooks.com/physical

Now, if you enjoyed the book you just read, please leave a positive review of it where you bought it (e.g. Amazon). It'll help get it out there a lot more and mean I can continue writing these books for you. So thank you. :)

www.SaucyRomanceBooks.com/RomanceBooks

More Books By Shannon Gardener

If you liked this, you'll love Sharron Gardener's other Christian romance stories such as 'Faith' (search 'Faith Sharron Gardener' on Amazon to get it now). Here's the description and a sample:

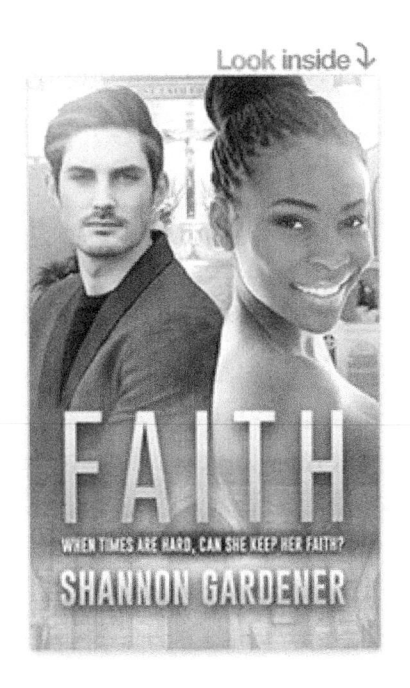

Description:

A Christian romance for adults.

www.SaucyRomanceBooks.com/RomanceBooks

Faith is a woman of the church who is down on her luck.

Still feeling the affect of her mother's premature passing, job cuts and the prospect of no work has brought her close to breaking point.

Now she risks losing her faith.

After all, she has a direct line to God, and he's supposed to listen to her. Instead, her life has gone from bad to worse...

… but not all is lost.

Enter Joshua, a man who has been sent at the right time to get Faith back on her feet.

With the prospect of a new job and a man worthy of her love, will it be enough to help regain her faith?

Find out in this new Christian romance by Shannon Gardener.

Suitable for over 18s only due to sexual scenes between a God loving couple.

Sample:

She bawled. There was no better way to put it and to describe the way the tears were coming fast and furious. She had felt it inside her spirit. There had been talks about layoffs, downsizing and letting go but she had allowed herself to hope and she had prayed; after all she had a direct line to God and he was supposed to listen to her.

She had kept everything in and had even managed to smile and nod when they told her they were so sorry to let her go but she understood: 'last in first out' and it wasn't that she was not doing a good job; as a matter of fact she was doing an excellent job and she had gotten the beautiful recommendation letters to prove it and the two weeks check that would be sent in the mail.

Faith wiped her hand over her wet cheeks, furtively looking if anyone was noticing her breakdown – she was a private person and did not allow people to see her unhinged, other than her mother, God bless her soul. She had a feeling that her troubles had started two years ago when her mother had been diagnosed with breast cancer; then everything had started declining. Her father had died when she was only nine years old so it had been just her and her mother for the past fifteen years.

She had thought that she was getting back on her feet and was living a normal life again and she had thrown herself into her work. She had done such a good job of it – getting in earlier than everyone and staying later than most. So much for that – after five years of being settled in a job she was now going to job hunt again.

With a sigh, she took up her box she had piled her personal stuff in and stood up to leave.

"Hey, Faith wait up," the voice sounded from behind her and she closed her eyes briefly, chiding herself that she had not left long ago and dealt with her self-pity behind closed doors. Pasting a smile on her face she turned towards Howard; one of the guys who worked beside her in the office.

"Hi Howard, I was just leaving," she told him pointedly. Ever since they had been working together at the company, he had been trying to get her to go out with him. His lanky frame came closer to her; his chocolate brown complexion a little flushed from his apparent run from the office building to catch her.

"I am glad I caught you," he told her a little breathlessly; either not getting that she wanted to leave or totally ignoring it. "Now that you're no longer working here, how about we start going out?" he grinned at her, his white smile a little crooked.

Faith stared at him in disbelief. She had just had her world turned upside down and here was this man asking her to go out with him and that's the only thing he can think to ask.

Taking a deep breath before she answered, with a quick flash she realized that her mother would have been so proud of her; as she was always telling her to take deep breaths before she spoke as words cannot be withdrawn once they are spoken. "I am sorry Howard, the answer is still no and I need to go home and consider my options; so if you'll excuse me," she started to move away from him but he held on to her arm.

"Hey, I can take care of you. A beautiful girl like you should not have to worry about where the next cent is coming from." He made an attempt at being charming.

Faith went rigid. The man was totally clueless and she felt like punching him in the unknown. "I am not one of those women who thinks she can use the assets God gave her to make a buck and I really resent that you think I might be." She told him frostily, pulling away her arm.

"Hey babes, please don't be that way," he protested trailing behind her as she made her way to her small beat up car. "I didn't mean to offend you; I was just looking out for you. I am worried about you babes, I don't want to know that you are out there wanting for anything."

Faith pulled her car door open and slide into the seat. "That's not on you Howard, I have a God whose job it is to take care of my needs," she put the car into reverse and without waiting for his response started backing out of the parking lot.

"Will he also take care of your physical needs?" he shouted. "You don't know what you're missing baby." He added, using his hands to cup his private area in a lewd gesture.
Faith shook her head in wonder and went on her way. She had reached a few blocks before she pulled off the road and started laughing hysterically. She had lost her job and being propositioned by the office 'lothario' in almost the same breath. What a pretty awful day. Leaning against the steering wheel she sighed wearily as she took a stock of her

circumstances; it certainly felt as if God had forgotten about her.

*****

As soon as she got home to the small house, she kicked off her shoes wearily and sank back into the well-worn settee. It was well past six o'clock but she was not in the least bit hungry; she had left overs from yesterday and usually on Fridays she would buy something from the restaurant across from where she worked but now she would have to pinch every penny because she did not know when next she would be earning a salary.

The house was small and an inheritance from her mother, thank God. So she did not have to worry about paying rent or a mortgage as her mother had paid off her house a long time ago. Her gaze went over to where a large portrait hung over the small fireplace, her mother smiled gently down at her; a serenely peaceful expression on her face. She had gotten her looks from her mother who had always told her teasingly that she looked like a black Barbie doll. She unconsciously passed a hand over her riot of curls that framed her small oval face. She had been asked more times than she could count by men who worked alongside her and even those in upper management but she had remained firm in her answer; she never dated anyone she worked with – too many complications could ensue. She had seen it happen many times in the office and how uncomfortable the atmosphere had gotten after it had turned sour. And her mother had told her never to settle. "You're a beautiful girl, my dear; so let it be that you are in love with the person you allow to enter into your space and consider you will be spending the rest of your life with him and make sure that God approves; because being trapped in a loveless marriage has got to be the most awful thing in the world. Contrary to what society says, we as women, don't need a man to take care of us. I loved your father and he was all I needed and when he died I was not interested in anyone else."

Her phone rang just then and from the caller id she found out it was her friend Maureen. "I really hope you are not at home wallowing in self-pity and thinking that all is lost," she said firmly. "We know that when one door is closed God opens another one."

Faith rolled her eyes. She and Maureen had been best friends since they were teenagers at the same school and attending the same church. They had been through a lot together and she had been a shoulder to cry on when Maureen's husband had filed for divorce two years ago. Now she was dating a wonderful man who would do anything for her. "Mark and I were wondering if you want to come to dinner with us tomorrow night."

"Does every sentence begin with 'Mark and I' now?" Faith teased; momentarily forgetting her woes.

"Not all the time," Maureen retorted. "But most of the time. How about it? Dinner tomorrow night?"

"No," Faith refused gently. "Saturdays are date nights for you and I am going to be updating my resume so I will be too busy to be wallowing in self-pity."

"Well I am coming over tonight," the girl said decidedly and Faith could almost see her getting ready to leave the house.

"Maureen please," Faith laughingly protested. "I will be going to bed shortly and I already had my crying jog so it's out of my system." She told her friend about her crying on the steps of her workplace and the weird encounter she had with Howard from work.

"I hope you told him where to put his suggestion," Maureen said heatedly.

"No, seeing as I am a good Christian girl, I was very polite." Faith said with a laugh. "And besides I will see you at church on Sunday."

"Are you sure you are okay?" Maureen asked in concern.

"Not really, but I will be." Faith told her and she meant it.

"Okay love," Maureen said. "I have some papers to mark before I get my beauty sleep." She was a Junior High school teacher.

After she had hung up from Maureen, Faith went into the tiny kitchen to get something to eat – all of sudden she had gotten her appetite back. Maureen was right, she would find something else very soon – she was not named 'Faith' for nothing; she would not let a little thing like losing her job make her think that all was over. It certainly was not.

*****

Her Saturdays were usually spent doing housework but since she did not have a job to go to come Monday morning, she could afford to put off doing laundry for a day. She was going to update her resume and make sure it was eye-catching enough to get her employed. She was a trained secretary and was very good at what she did and she was going to make sure someone out there knew it; she was a catch in the business world. Months after her mother had died, she still had not found the energy or inclination to clear out her stuff. It was Maureen who had gently persuaded that her mother's clothes and few pieces of jewelry that she herself did not want was better served if they were given to people in need. So she had turned her bedroom into a small study and had moved into her mother's bedroom. Now to get to work, she thought with determination, booting up her lap top.

It was almost one o'clock when she stirred from the small scarred desk she had found at a garage sale and stood up, stretching her tired muscles. She had not bothered to change out of her pajamas and she grimaced as she remembered that her mother would have scolded her for being in night wear at this time of day. "Life is a dress rehearsal, darling. No matter what is going on with us, we get up take a shower and get ready to meet the day and that means getting rid of our yesterdays and starting a fresh day – you never know what possibilities it holds."

Faith went into the bathroom and took a quick shower, barely glancing into the mirror to look at her coffee and cream complexion; noticing that her large chocolate brown eyes were a little too bright. She had often been told of her beauty but it meant little or nothing to her and even though she dressed well; she did not go through any extra effort.

She went into the kitchen to fix something; remembering that she had poured herself some coffee and had gulped it down hot before going into the study to deal with her resume. Her stomach rumbled as she pulled out corned beef and made a huge sandwich; some hot chocolate and a glass of orange juice. Her mother had always told her that after a very good breakfast one can always conquer the world. She dug around in the kitchen drawer to find a recipe book her mother had made over the years; it had been so long since she had cooked herself a very good meal and she thought she would do so today. Why not? She might as well cook a good meal now, who knows when she would be able to afford another one? It was then she found it. The Bible her mother always kept in the kitchen. She always called it 'the kitchen Bible' and she would always take it out whenever she was cooking, along with her recipe book and read scriptures. Faith sat down on the stool at the kitchen counter with the 'Good book' and thumbed through it; smiling wistfully at the many red and yellow highlights of particular chapters she wanted to remember. There were many times when they had spent time inside the warmth of this kitchen; she sitting and watching while her mother measured and poured and stirred and when she was old enough she had done some of the measuring and pouring and there had always been love and laughter and contentment. Her mother had told her the story of when she had met her father and how very shy he had been and she had broken through his reserves. Faith had wanted to hear the story over and over again and her mother had always humored her by repeating it every time she had asked. She had told her that one day the Lord would provide a man for her who was going to be her husband and that there was no need to rush anything – it will all be there at the right time.

She thumbed through the well-worn pages; her eyes brimming with tears. She missed her so much that sometimes she wondered if she was ever going to go on without her. They had shared everything and had spent so much time just being friends. With a decisive sniff she put the Bible on the counter and started to prepare something to eat; she was not going to be miserable today; she had to try and be happy even if she had to force herself.

www.SaucyRomanceBooks.com/RomanceBooks

*****

The Baptist church she had grown up in was not big – in fact it was more of a family gathering where everyone knew each other and was always deeply involved in each other's lives. Faith parked the car in the parking lot and headed towards the building; a determined smile on her beautiful face. She had dressed for success this morning. The weather was summery even though it was spring and she had chosen to wear a red and white cotton dress with small cap sleeves and white heels; her hair bundled on top of her head with several curls rioting on her cheeks. She had no intention of unburdening herself to all and sundry; church family or not. Her mother had taught her to take her burdens to the Lord and let him deal with it – self-pity is not allowed. She smiled at the Barber family who were also on their way in and waved to old Mrs. Elliot who had lost her husband and son ten years ago in a terrible car accident; the woman positively radiated faith and hope and refused to blame God for anything. "God knows best," she had said firmly. "Who am I to question Him?" Faith wished she could view things like that but she was far way from being at that place.

Maureen and Mark came in shortly after and sat beside her. Faith liked Mark; he was very unassuming and quiet and loved Maureen very much. He was tall and lanky and wore glasses. He had a light brown complexion and hazel eyes and Maureen called him her almost white guy. "You look great for someone who is unemployed." Maureen commented dryly.

"Look good, feel good," Faith whispered with a smile. Maureen had always told her friend that her beauty was almost unreal and she made people like her looked frumpy.

"Honey you don't have to make any extra effort to do so," Maureen whispered as Pastor Baker climbed the simple wooden pulpit.

His sermon was on starting over and Faith listened with interest as the man told his congregation that sometimes people are forced to adapt to changes but God has a plan for every person and every situation in one's lives.

The service was finished with the choir singing 'All to Jesus I Surrender' and Pastor Baker making his usual plea for the congregation to totally rely on God, who knows what the future holds.

It was more than half an hour before they were able to go outside because of the traditional meet and greet that takes place after every service.

"My dear, how are you holding up?" Pastor Baker came over just as she was about to leave.

"I am holding on pastor," Faith said with a smile. She had always respected and like the elderly man who paid so much attention to matters of the soul.

"I hope you know that if there is anything you need, you can always come to me," he told her sincerely, his brow creased with concern. "Your dear mother was such a blessing to us all and I miss her every day."

For a minute Faith had to fight back the tears that threatened to come but with a brace of her narrow shoulders she smiled slightly. "I know Pastor, she will always be missed."

"God bless you my dear," he said kindly, patting her hand gently before moving away to greet some other congregates.

She hurried outside to find Maureen and Mark who were waiting beside her car. Mark's car was parked alongside hers and Faith smiled as she saw that they were holding hands. "How adorable," she teased, her eyes twinkling.

"Thanks," Maureen said flippantly. "We are going to grab some food at 'Eda's'" she told her friend; referring to a local restaurant a few blocks away. "And we are not taking no for an answer."

"Yes mother," Faith said dryly. "How do you put up with her bossiness?" she asked Mark, as she opened her car door in readiness to get in.

"I love her too much to wonder about that," Mark said with his slow smile creasing his attractive face.

"Good answer," Maureen said fondly, pecking his cheek as they turned and went towards his car. "See you there," she waved at Faith.

'Eda's eatery' was a small local restaurant that catered and was famous for its fried chicken, wild rice and vegetable casserole and on Sundays there was hardly any available seats. ""I have a table for you," plump and smiling Eda bustled over to them. She was a church member and always looked out for them. "How was church?"

"Very good," Maureen answered, taking a seat as soon as Mark pulled out her chair for her. It had taken her awhile to get used to Mark doing things like that for her. "What happened to you?"

"My Sunday help bailed on me," Eda shook her head. "I will have to get rid of that girl," she said regretfully.

She took their orders and bustled away, coming back shortly with steaming plates of food.

"So what's the plan?" Maureen asked, spooning some rice inside her mouth.

"Job hunting starting tomorrow," Faith said with a shrug. She did not have much appetite but gamely sliced off a piece of chicken.

"I was thinking that maybe you should give yourself some space," Maureen said softly. "Like get a week's rest before you start to hunt."

"I don't need rest Maureen, I need to be earning a living," Faith said a little sharply.

www.SaucyRomanceBooks.com/RomanceBooks

"All right honey, it was just a suggestion," the other girl said soothingly.

Faith shook her head and did not respond. It was Mark who changed the subject, regaling them with stories about a sales rep at his office. Very soon the mood had lightened and Faith found herself cleaning her plate and actually laughing. She was not going to let the problem overwhelm her.

*

Want to read the rest? Then search 'Faith Sharron Gardener' on Amazon to get it now...

You can also see other related books by myself and other top romance authors at:

www.saucyromancebooks.com/romancebooks

Made in United States
Orlando, FL
17 January 2024